Published in Great Britain by

LR Price Publications which is the trading name of

LR Publishing London Ltd

27 Old Gloucester Street,

London, WC1N 3AX

www.lrpricepublications.com

ISBN: 978-1-916613-38-6

Toxic Options

James Douglas-Mann

Dedication

To Michelle and Izzy

Chapter One

June 1983

Walthamstow High St was quiet now. In the early hours of Sunday morning, Joss poured his brother another scotch and emptied the remaining contents of the bottle into his own glass. As he raised the glass to his lips and swirled the oaky liquid around his mouth, he reflected that this was a much needed 'medicinal' treatment following the traumatic events of the previous night.

"It's at times like this you wish Ronnie and Reggie were still around," said his brother Wayne gloomily, referring to the gangsters who, thirty years earlier, had represented an unofficial version of the East End's Police Force.

Joss sighed deeply, put down his glass and peered around the room, away from the empty safe which should have been concealing over £100,000 in used bank notes, except for the unfortunate set of events that had transpired a mere two hours earlier.

Joss and Wayne Archer were Turf Accountants, more commonly known as bookmakers, and the previous evening they had enjoyed their finest ever Saturday night at the White City Stadium, the home of Greyhound racing, which each year hosted the final of the Greyhound Derby. The Greyhound Derby was the dog racing equivalent of horse racing's Royal Ascot, and on this June evening, as it was every year, the Shepherds Bush stadium had been packed to the rafters with punters and fans from every walk of life across the social spectrum. This included working men, couples, stag parties, office parties, celebrities and, as Wayne liked to call them, "hoorays". This referred to the new breed of enthusiasts from Chelsea, simply known as 'the City' to most, that seemed to have only just discovered that there existed an alternative form of gambling to either the sport of kings or the green baize of the Casino. The sport was in its heyday, and its popularity even on an average Saturday night was almost back to levels not seen since the golden age of dog racing in between the last two world wars.

Joss and Wayne owned the number one pitch at White City. It was so called because its location gave the brothers access to the largest number of punters, being situated not only on the first row of the four lines of bookmakers occupying pitches, but also being in the middle of the front line directly facing the main stand. The reality, however, was that the location of the brothers' pitch may just have well been an irrelevance, such was the reputation of the Turf Accountants Archer. The brothers' pitch stood out amongst their rival bookmakers like a shining beacon. Whereas their rivals were a motley collection of surly old men who had been in the trade for most of their lives and worked to safe, slender margins, the Archers themselves had only been in business for five years and would accept the size of bets and liabilities that their rivals only shuddered at. Not that they needed to, but Joss and Wayne wanted the public to know that they were "the men". So vociferous were they, that during a night's racing either could have been taken for a stand-up comedian playing to a large audience.

"Come on now, who wants a wager? Six-to-four the field," Joss would boom, donned in his loud white suit and voluminous gold jewellery, whilst Wayne would drag on an enormous Cuban cigar and add, "Alright, 'oorays allowed as well. Where are the yuppies tonight -still quaffing bubbly at Royal Ascot?"

The crowd would laugh and trade banter with the two brothers before the serious business of wagering came to hand, at which time punters would scour the betting ring seeking the best value, usually settling on Joss and Wayne, whose prices on the better fancied dogs were generally bigger than those offered by their rather staid opposition. The punters loved them because they added to the overall experience, and on a good night from a bookmaker's perspective, where most of the favourites were beaten, Joss and Wayne would regularly take profits of £20,000-£30,000 whilst remaining good humoured on the occasional bad nights when the 'jollies' kept winning.

Part of the appeal of the intrepid brothers was the curious question of how they had come to be bookmakers in the first place. Both men were in their late forties, and one of the tabloids had recently run a feature on Wayne entitled *How My Career Went to the Dogs*, an article referring to his past life as a chartered accountant and how he'd swapped audits and non-stop business meetings for a smoky betting shop in East London and evenings juggling the odds at a handful of London Greyhound Stadiums.

Nobody seemed to know much about Joss, not that it appeared to prevent speculation.

"I 'eard 'e spent arf 'is life in the nick," was one commonly vaunted comment.

"He was a failed comedian," was another popular theme.

The previous evening's fifty-third running of the Daily Mirror Greyhound Derby had proved to be the high point of Joss and Wayne's bookmaking careers to date. That morning they'd scratched a few buttons from the morning meeting at Hackney Wick before returning to the shop in Walthamstow in the afternoon, where they'd gratefully watched winning outsiders run riot at the last day of the Royal Ascot meeting.

"Like pilgrims on the way to Mecca," was how Joss had described themselves as they had set off for White City in the late afternoon, driven by their clerk Colin. He and Wayne shared the onerous responsibility of booking literally thousands of bets in the course of a major evening such as this, but whilst Colin's duties were merely to drive and do clerical duties, Wayne's role was of a more academic nature, given that his calculating and analytical mind framed the odds that adorned the Archer's blackboard. If Wayne was the academic, Joss was the showman, and as soon as he had chalked up the prices of the six canine contestants in a race the banter would commence, an ever-widening throng of punters circling the Archer stand.

Full of anticipation, the trio had arrived at White City shortly before six o'clock, where they parked their series five BMW in the large car park. The pilgrims were certainly expecting to reap some treasure that night. The first of fifteen races on this particular June evening had started at 6:27pm, and was followed every fifteen minutes by another, except in the case of the Derby final itself, which required twenty-five minutes breathing space either side in order to give the television coverage more time to cover the form and profiles of each contender, and an extended period after the big race in which to interview the winning connections.

Right from the start of the evening's sport the results had gone the brothers' way, the fate of each favourite turned to dust. A sea of groans and boos emerged from the stands as in each race the favourite would either be baulked, knocked over, trip over hurdles, or get pipped in the tightest of photograph finishes. The punters were getting to the point where they may have even been out of the stadium and on the tube home had it not been Derby night, but as the minutes to the big event ticked by it was becoming very clear that the favourite in Trap Six was going to attract colossal support. The creature in question was a tall and handsome black beast running from his favoured berth on the outside and over his optimum distance of five hundred meters. The animal had devastated all opposition in the qualifying rounds over the previous eight weeks and had easily the best time figures out of his five rivals. All the big bookmaking chains had earlier installed him as a burning hot eight to eleven favourite. Excitement on the track had reached fever pitch as the six dogs paraded in front of the teeming stands and were led by their handlers around the track to the starting traps.

"Backing odds on favourites is not for widows and orphans," Joss had shouted out, fully aware that the majority of the hardened element of his client base would soon be piling on the favourite and supposed 'good thing' as if defeat was out of the question. The hardened element had been rather larger than Joss had anticipated as he eyed them gathering with menace around the pitch, but he had deliberately held off quoting a price until Colin had returned from his surveillance exercise of the other bookmakers' prices – particularly the price of the favourite in Trap Six.

"Ok you lot, not long now! Ye of little faith," Joss belted out. "You're like whores you lot –You're getting fucked every fifteen minutes!" he teased.

"Come on Joss. I'll get on with Dave Little if you don't 'urry up," shouted one punter.

Colin eventually returned to the pitch with the comparative odds as the dogs and their handlers made their way to only a few yards behind the starting traps. The prices he handed Wayne on the 'Six Dog' were even shorter than the brothers had anticipated, with a four-to-six chance being most common. Only a couple of the bigger players offered the slightly more generous price of eight-to-eleven, matching the ante post prices of the big chains earlier in the week. An astute onlooker might have noticed Wayne wink at Joss and briefly wiggle his right forefinger up and down in one single motion.

"Alright then you lot, not all at once," John chuckled before chalking a small dash by the name of Trap Six on his black board. "Evens Six!" After a few moments of disbelief from incredulous punters wondering if something had gone amiss with the most celebrated dog in the competition, the crowd had caved in on the Archer pitch, literally flooding them with bets. The brothers operated a £10 minimum bet policy on major nights such as this, but few of the thousand odd wagers they recorded over the ensuing minutes were small as that. They took fifties, hundreds, and thousands, the largest being an even eight thousand pounds from an unknown customer wearing a dinner jacket, as was required on Derby night by diners in the club restaurant. Four figure bets were plentiful on the favourite, particularly from rival bookies eager to hedge their own potential liabilities.

"Fuck me bro, we're up to our necks with this one," murmured Wayne. Joss hardly needed telling as he produced a cloth and erased the six dogs' prices from the board before turning towards the track to watch their fate.

At last, the announcer's voice had crackled over the loudspeaker to proclaim "The harrrrrrrrrre's runnnnnning," and the noise volume in the stands abated eerily for a few seconds. As the hare flew past the awaiting traps and the iron gates sprung aloft, the six greyhounds hurtled towards the first bend amidst the famous 'Derby Roar' as the White City crowd screamed their encouragement. The roar was as loud as ever that year as swinging round the first bend, a length in front, was the favourite in Trap Six. By the second bend the lead had been extended to two lengths, and by the time the dogs were rounding the third the decibel and excitement level emanating from the crowd had reached fever pitch. And it was at the fourth and final bend on the track that either the strain of being labelled 'the champion elect' for eight weeks, or the sudden loss of ardour at staring at a hare's backside, or perhaps because he'd simply just run out of puff, that the 'Six', the darling of the nation's punters, had found his stride shortening and was left floundering as traps One and Two passed him two yards from the line.

Joss, Wayne, and Colin had returned hurriedly to the car park the minute that they had settled the last winning ticket after the final race. Under his arm, Colin carried the ledger board that recorded each bet struck throughout the night. Later, scrutiny of that board would show that the Archer brothers had had their finest ever evening, netting around £100,000 in profit. Joss and Wayne had one hand each on their satchel, almost bursting at the seams with booty. Both men were painfully aware that this was far too much money to be carrying around a none too salubrious area of West London.

The trio had reached the four door BMW without incident, Colin sitting himself in the driver's seat with Joss and Wayne in the back, either side of the satchel. Having exited the car park and entered nearby Wood Lane, the three men's nerves abated and they started whooping with delight as they inhaled the success of the night's proceedings.

"Not a bad night to do that on, eh?" said Wayne.

"And we're safe," added Colin. In the dark of night, Colin hadn't noticed the white Ford transit that carefully followed the BMW's every move through Kensington, Knightsbridge, Piccadilly, Holborn, The City, and Mile End, where Colin eventually turned into

Southern Grove.

Southern Grove was a leafy, long, and quiet road with a graveyard on one side and a council estate on the other. Towards the end of the road Colin had slowed the car to a halt, and, with the engine still running, handed the keys to Wayne. The three men high fived and clapped each other on the back before finally Colin disappeared down an alleyway towards his flat. Wayne replaced him in the driver's seat with Joss remaining in the back with the satchel full of pilgrim's treasure.

Thirty yards away from the blackness, four hidden pairs of eyes surveyed the scene unfold with avid interest. On the remainder of the journey home, the brothers dissected their most triumphant races of the evening and Joss called his wife Ann from an extraordinary contraption known as a mobile phone. This latest product of scientific research and development was known as The Motorola and was the size of a house brick. Joss loved it, not just for its obvious convenience, but for the undoubted badge of loud confidence that it represented. He knew that his call would probably wake Ann, but he'd promised to phone her on the way back, especially if the likelihood was that he'd be late, and late they were going to be given that they had the little matter of having to dump £100,000 somewhere secure, specifically the safe in the office above their betting shop on Walthamstow High St.

Twenty-five minutes after leaving Southern Grove they were on Walthamstow High St. Wayne noted how different it was at this time of night when the market was silent and defunct –so unlike during the day when it resembled a busy betting ring with market traders shouting the odds to their own punters, the shopping public. He mused that by now even the ring at White City would be silent like this.

Two minutes later Wayne brought the car to a halt and managed to park just outside the betting shop halfway down the hill. As were the rules in the eighties, the public were not permitted to see through the windows of licensed premises, and as such the outside of the shop displayed darkened glass with a sign in the front which read *Archer Bros, est. 1978.* Joss had decided to add 'est. 1978' as befitted his sense of humour, given that the business was only five years old. Underneath the sign were handwritten sheets and a selection of odds on the forthcoming football season's outright winners of the topflight, League Division One, reading *3/1 Liverpool, 4/1 Man Utd, 5/1 Newcastle, 8/1 Leeds.*

Wayne turned off the ignition and opened the side door of the BMW. He fished in a coat pocket for the keys to the shop, slammed shut the car door and entered the keys into the latch. The familiar high pitched warning signal from the burglar alarm whistled as Wayne walked briskly through the unlit shop towards the cupboard behind the counter to turn off the alarm, leaving the door of the shop ajar and his brother behind him. Groaning as he heaved himself from the back seat of the BMW, Joss cursed at the weight of the money-laden satchel as he staggered with the case towards the open door of the shop.

Just before he reached the entrance he paused, looking at the handwritten odds on display in the window.

"We're a bit big on Leeds, aren't we bruv?" said Joss. He didn't get to hear Wayne's reply.

It had all happened in a few seconds. As Wayne had switched off the burglar alarm, he was suddenly troubled that he hadn't noticed Joss enter the shop. Then he heard the thud outside. With sudden, mounting panic, Wayne feared the worst and strode stealthily yet cautiously towards the open door. He saw a figure at the entrance; not Joss, but a man wearing a Mrs Thatcher mask, making his intentions reasonably clear by the four-foot-long baseball bat in his right hand.

Wayne lunged towards the intruder, now petrified for the safety of his brother – not to mention the contents of the satchel. He didn't see Joss, who lay unconscious by the window under the chart which read *League Division One. Be on target and bet with Archers.*

A second and third man, their faces also covered by Mrs Thatcher masks, seemed to appear from nowhere, although Wayne later realised that they had likely emerged from the alleyway at the side of the shop.

A voice that he certainly didn't recognise growled at Wayne in a thick Northern Irish accent. "Cool it, Archer, while you toerags still have your lives, if not your money."

Wayne stopped in his tracks and turned in the direction of the voice. He ended up staring straight down the barrels of two sawn-off shotguns, one held by each of the two new assailants.

"What have you..." Wayne's voice petered off as he noticed his brother on the ground, now beginning to come round. There was no sign of the bag of money.

Hesitantly, the gunmen started edging backwards, the barrels of the shotguns still trained on Wayne. Having reversed ten paces, the gunmen finally turned their backs and broke into a sprint down the hill, swiftly followed by the man with the baseball bat. Before they had covered forty yards, a white Ford transit van screeched alongside the masked robbers, and the men hastily clambered in. The van screamed into a U-turn and sped back up the hill, passing Wayne and the now recovering Joss. As it sailed by, Wayne saw the large bag in the arms of the man in the passenger seat, who appeared to be the Prime Minister. The Prime Minister managed to throw up his two fingers in a V-sign at Wayne as the van made its getaway and disappeared over the hill. Wayne just caught sight of the number plate.

"Who the fuck's just ruined our big night bruv?" croaked Joss, clutching his head.

"Dunno," said Wayne, his face buried in his hands.

"I'm even money we find 'em. Let's go and have a drink," said Joss.

Chapter Two

August 1986

Sir Marcus Holderness still caught the Central line to the City every day. He amused himself by remembering Thatcher's famous gaffe in the eighties, when she'd remarked "Anyone who still uses public transport in their thirties hasn't made it in life." Marcus wasn't bothered. The central line was a two-minute walk from his rather grand house in Notting Hill, and it took him a mere thirty-five minutes from his front door to the London Stock Exchange. Notting Hill Gate to Bank by tube was much more convenient than using his driver, and it gave him a sense of pride that he still had the common touch.

Marcus had certainly made it in life anyway. After Eton he'd worked briefly on a sheep ranch in Australia before taking his place at Cambridge to study Economics. A 2-1, or a 'gentleman's degree', as his mother had described it, had ensued, followed by National Service. After that he'd disagreed with his barrister father about going into law and had chosen to work for a small firm of stockbrokers called Edwin James and co. instead. Here he started life as a 'blue button', the absolute lowest of the low, and despite his somewhat privileged background he was happy to carry bags, write up stock prices on Edwin James and co.'s board on the Exchange, deliver messages, and most importantly of all take the partners breakfast orders each morning.

Marcus was always the first in The Box, which was the name of the room within the Exchange where the dealing staff at Edwin

James and co. spent the trading hours as a base when not on the floor itself. Then, when the London market officially closed at 3.30 in the afternoon, the dealing staff returned to their office in Moorgate.

Marcus was a diligent junior. Respect for his fellow men, irrespective of their background, had been instilled into him during his National Service at Catterick Barracks, and whilst he'd been lucky enough to escape World War Two by a mere few years, his Regimental Sergeant Major, a hard and unforgiving Welshman, had pushed Marcus to his mental and physical limits. This education had made Marcus well equipped to gain respect, make friends easily, and be a diligent worker.

After two years working in The Box, Marcus had been given a choice. He could either have graduated to a 'yellow button', an authorised dealer permitted to take orders from clients, or he could move away from the intensity of the dealing environment and become more involved in the research side of his employer's business. Marcus opted for the latter, and it wasn't long before his analytical mind was producing research papers that were not only the envy of his colleagues but had got him noticed by some of the larger City firms.

His reputation soon outgrew Edwin James and co., and in his early thirties Marcus moved both company and job, joining Sinclair's Merchant Bank, in their Corporate Finance department. In spite of numerous offers from rival merchant banks and venture capitalists, Marcus was loyal to Sinclair's, and there he remained for the duration of his Corporate Finance career.

Over the years, he witnessed various booms and recessions

come and go, either of which he thrived on, advising either predatory companies on their intended takeover targets or vulnerable companies on how to maintain their independence when caught in the headlights of an unwanted suitor.

Marcus retired shortly after his fiftieth birthday, having received his knighthood for 'services to business.' Some of the nations' most noted Captains of Industry were at his retirement dinner, hosted by Marcus, his wife Diana, and their two sons. The plaudits and speeches went on long into the night, and Marcus reflected gratefully on a successful career whilst looking forward to a long and happy retirement.

Retirement, however, did not come easily to Sir Marcus. He'd never had much time for golf and his shooting was poor, no matter how many lessons he took. He'd never really accustomed himself to the country or it's related sporting pursuits, and apart from taking a month with Diana in their villa in the South of France, Marcus's time was predominantly spent in the house in Notting Hill studying the movements of world markets and preparing for numerous company meetings of which he was on the board. Within two years of his new 'idyllic' life, Marcus was bored rigid and beginning to get on his family's nerves. His sons used to be driven to mock despair when Marcus would say "There's no way I can go back now, I'm too old and-nobody would have me."

One day a letter dropped through the box at his spacious Notting Hill residence. It was an invitation to lunch at the London Stock Exchange, and Marcus had to wonder if there was an agenda.

"No such thing as a free lunch, y'know," he announced to his long-suffering family.

He was right. During the lunch, the Chairman of the Stock Exchange had invited Marcus to take up an appointment as head of the Regulatory and Supervision committee. Marcus had protested that his experience was not befitting of such a role ('it was rather like poacher turning gamekeeper,' he thought) but the Chairman had no such doubts. He explained to Marcus that it was a figurehead that he wanted; a mind that could adapt to any of the numerous different circumstances that could lead to stock exchange rules being breached. There had been a spate of insider dealing offences recently, and the government was pressing the stock exchange to take preventative measures by way of securing evidence that may lead to prosecutions.

To the undoubted relief of his family, Marcus accepted the role and was bequeathed a magnificent office on the twenty-third floor of the London Stock Exchange. A breathtaking view was to be had over Threadneedle Street and beyond, and Marcus settled quickly into his new role, acquainting himself with his new department by inviting the whole twenty-person team for drinks in his office one evening.

The members of the team were comprised mainly of accountants, lawyers, and information technology experts, but also a couple of ex-policemen, several ex-compliance officers, and two young members of stock exchange staff who otherwise performed general duties. Marcus wasn't sure at first what 'general duties' meant, but he soon discovered that their role within the Regulatory and Supervision Department was to act as intelligence officers from the disguise of their administrative jobs on the market floor.

Marcus made his way as usual from Bank Station into Throgmorton Street and through the large double doors of the stock exchange, greeting old friends as he went, mainly stockbrokers and stockjobbers about to resume another day's battle on the floor. The stockbrokers took the orders from their clients and the stockjobbers facilitated those orders, quoting a two-way price, one to buy and the other to sell, on either of which the stockbrokers could deal.

There was a major new issue today, an offering of stock in a newly quoted public company which had recently been denationalised by the Conservative government, a decision which was preceded by a massive television campaign to persuade the public to invest in shares. Today would attract plentiful media interest and see mayhem on the floor of the exchange as jobbers were almost knocked over in the rush as eager brokers strove to deal at the best prices. Share prices were booming in general, and the press were speculating that this 'bull market' had a long way to go.

Sir Marcus felt a pang of envy as he walked past the floor and stood by the lift, remembering those happy days as a 'blue button' at Edwin James and co. He heard the bell ring and a crescendo of noise as the brokers ran onto the floor towards the jobbers, waiting with their books open, rooted to their pitches like soldiers defending their position. These pitches were large hexagonal boxes that protruded from the floor, with updated prices marked by the name of each stock.

The morning passed in typical fashion. Marcus received his coffee and the morning papers from his secretary, and as he flicked through the financial news he made the occasional note of unusual share price movements and press comment that referred to 'speculative buying or selling' that had led to any sharp rises or declines in stock values. At eleven he attended a meeting that outlined the progress the department were having with ongoing investigations, and he was made to feel rather old as one of the young IT wizards demonstrated the complex new technology his team were using to detect price anomalies. After the meeting Marcus returned to his office and returned Diana's call reminding him that they were supposed to be attending The Royal Court Theatre in Sloane Square that night for Caryl Churchill's new play, *Serious Money*. Marcus wondered whether it contained any fraud.

Marcus was just about to leave for lunch with Brian Perry, a longstanding friend and market legend who was a partner in one of the large jobbing firms on the exchange floor, when his secretary knocked on the door. She stepped into the room and placed a large brown folder on his desk. The folder had an envelope attached with the words *London Stock Exchange, Strictly Private and Confidential* written on it. It was marked *For the attention of Sir Marcus Holderness*.

Marcus opened the envelope and was surprised to see that the note inside was handwritten by one of his senior accountants. It simply read:

Dear Sir Marcus,

I hope that one of the names on the enclosed list doesn't cause you any unnecessary embarrassment. We are merely at an exploratory level of investigation at this stage anyway.

Kind regards, Alan.

With mounting curiosity, and more than a little concern, Marcus laid his umbrella back on his desk. Brian could wait a few minutes.

From the folder he removed a thick computer print-out with itemised records of hundreds of trades and their relevant counterparties. They made little sense to him as he flicked through the green and white sheets, but he then noticed an unattached memo with a list of individual names, together with the name of the bank, stockbroker or stockjobbing firms that each name worked for. These were listed in alphabetical order.

None of the names made much sense to him as he cast his eye down the list. Davis, Drysdale, Fuente, Grossmith, Henderson, Hill, Jackson, Johnson, Michaels, Norris, Perry........ Perry? Marcus doubled back and observed with relief that the corresponding initial was not B, and thus did not implicate his friend. The potential culprit's employer however was of very real concern.

He looked again. The letters in front of him read, Perry, D., Sinclair Bank.

"Daniel Perry?" he said aloud. Brian's son. The same Daniel Perry that Marcus had found a job for in his last year at Sinclair's.

Having lunch with the boy's father today was not a happy coincidence. Marcus decided not to mention anything to Brian. It was too early to make any accusations, and besides, Marcus didn't really understand the full nature of the alleged offences at this stage anyway. All he did know was that they looked potentially serious, but he would just have to try and make the most of lunch and try to discuss other matters more jovial.

They had agreed to meet in *The Long Room*, a popular grill in Throgmorton Street favoured by brokers and jobbers. Marcus's highbrow fellow committee members wouldn't be seen dead there, but Marcus had always enjoyed the buzz that came from within, and the sense of humour which was unique to the majority of regulars that convened, some every day, for gin and tonics followed by steak and chips, cheese, red wine and for some, port or calvados for afters.

Brian was in typically ebullient form as he bragged about the successful trading positions his dealers had enjoyed that morning.

"We were five million quid long of stock coming in this morning, double that by elevenses, but now those pikey brokers can't get enough of it. Every time I mark a price up, even more buyers appear."

Marcus laughed with his old pal. He and Brian had been blue

buttons together in the old days and shared many of the same stock exchange friends. He wondered uncomfortably if that had anything to do with his appointment on the regulatory committee. Not that he had anything to feel awkward about in Brian's company. Brian Perry may have started life from less affluent roots, but integrity and honesty were Brian's trademarks, and Marcus trusted him to the hilt. Marcus was an excellent judge of character, a quality that had stood him in good stead throughout his career, and as he listened to his friend recount the latest tales of how he'd "cleaned up in Cable and Wireless" or the one about telling Alan Sugar that he'd "do all right with Amstrad", or the story of "Sweaty Betty" walking around the floor all day with a duster mischievously attached to the back of her skirt by some errant blue button, Marcus felt a deep sadness at the pain that his old pal might be facing were the Regulatory Department to pursue Daniel on insider dealing charges. He would need to think long and hard how to deal with this uncomfortable situation.

Back in his office Marcus looked through the file in detail. He pressed the buzzer to call in his secretary.

Toxic Options

Chapter Three

Late August 1896

Dan Perry was not in a good mood that Friday morning. He turned on each of the screens in front of him to see how the overnight markets had performed.

His daily routine was to leave his flat in Fulham at 7 am, pick up his copies of *The Sporting Life* and *The Financial Times*, and catch the number 14 bus to South Kensington before adjoining the Underground and taking the Circle Line to Liverpool Street. Once there, he could be at his desk at Sinclair Bank just a few minutes later, before the 8 am deadline for all the traders to be at their desks.

Dan felt the dryness in his throat and the sick feeling in his stomach. This was not so much due to the vast amount he'd drunk last night as it was the money he'd lost to those wretched bookmakers. The afternoon before had been a quiet one in the financial markets and appeared to present a good opportunity to get stuck into the racing on an above average weekday meeting at Newbury. Dan knew inwardly that the quality of the fare didn't really make much difference to him. He'd even started having large bets on greyhounds. And then there were the Friday nights when his mates and he congregated at The Crispin after work, a pub close to Sinclair Bank, and would play a mindless game called shoot pool which involved turning over the top of a set of coins having had ever increasing sized bets on whether the outcome would be head or tails. These games, always fuelled by a river of lager, inevitably got out of hand with someone writing out cheques for far more than they could realistically afford. Maybe he'd recover some of his recent gambling losses that night. He felt he was owed it.

In the background, Dan heard an analyst droning on about Marks and Spencer's figures, which had just been released.

"I'm recommending going overboard in the shares on the back of this statement," they said.

Dan was a trader and cared little for the academics who forecast the imminent destination of companies' share prices. His skill was to study changing share prices and act, often as not on instinct, speculating heavily with the Bank's money. That morning, Dan's mind was certainly not focused on the direction of the Marks and Spencer's share prices, instead drifting back to the previous night.

Having lost more than he felt comfortable with during the previous day's racing, it had seemed a good idea to round up some of his hardcore betting chums and visit Walthamstow dogs that night. The usual form was that they'd share a minicab to the track as soon as they could get out of the office, usually around 5.30 pm, then head straight for the bar. Over a few drinks they would study the card, a kind of analysis that Dan did approve of, before the first race was due off between 6.30 and 7.00.

One would say "Oh my God have you seen this 3 dog in the 7.29?" or "Do remember that dog's early pace, last time?" to the usual response of "Yeah, plenty of early but not enough late!"

The night before, they'd reached Walthamstow Stadium after the 45-minute drive in the minicab from the City. Dan always felt a shiver of excitement as the cab arrived in sight of the bright red neon lights saying *WELCOME TO WALTHAMSTOW, THE HOME OF GREYHOUND RACING* and next to it another smaller sign, *CHARLIE CHAN'S*, which was a nightclub popular amongst Essex partiers as well as various young City traders who only found themselves in there as a second thought, having spent the early hours of the night at the greyhound track.

That evening Dan had decided to up his stakes and had a major bet on a dog running towards the end of the night. He had a credit account with the Archer Brothers, who had the best pitch at the track, directly in front of the stand. They were two men in their late 40's who, whilst seeming perhaps a tad hard, never refused a bet of any size that Dan had ever seen, and had a good rapport with the crowd.

Tonight, Dan was planning on having his major bet with them. In fact, the brothers had even started to befriend Dan and his pals and tease them in a good-natured way. They had spotted that the best way to get hold of these City boys' money was to make the most noise, lay the most generous prices, and lay the largest bets. It was proving to be a sensible strategy, as a couple of months ago Joss Archer had offered to buy the 'Yuppies', as he called them, a drink, and invited them all to open credit accounts. Dan had asked how much credit they were being given and felt distinctly uneasy when Joss winked at him, saying "You don't have a credit limit son. We always get our money back in the end."

At 25 years of age, Dan had not had a credit account before.

He'd liked gambling since he was in his last two years at Lancing College, in Sussex. There was a day boy in his house who brought him a copy of *The Sporting Life* each day, and it was through that newspaper that he spotted advertisements from bookmakers offering deposit accounts. He always used to bet in considerably bigger size than his friends when he was 17, particularly whilst on illicit visits to racecourses, the likes of Brighton, Plumpton, Goodwood, and Fontwell, but getting access to large amounts of cash whilst at school was not that easy. He'd opened a deposit account with a firm called Guntrips, and during half-terms or holidays he'd top up the deposit account by sending Guntrips the cheque he was inevitably given by his parents.

Eight years later his circumstances had changed. His dad's friend Marcus Holderness had managed to get him into Sinclair Bank. Considering he hadn't been to university, Dan had thrived and risen from teaboy to trader within three years. As his seniority within the Bank increased so did his salary. They even paid him substantial bonuses. Dan decided that as his status had accelerated, it was time to have a proper credit account.

With the Archer Bros' unlimited credit account, Dan no longer had to worry himself about limiting his bets to the amount of cash he had in his pocket or lodged within his deposit accounts, of which he now had three, with Mecca Bookmakers and Heathorns having an account each, as well as the one with Guntrips. With deposit accounts there was the hassle of waiting for them to receive your cheque for funds, then wait yet more days for the cheque to clear before they accepted further bets. No, an unlimited credit account would be just ideal, and befit his new position as Senior Trader at Sinclair Bank.

With his mind now firmly focused on the first race, Dan recalled the £2,400 pounds he'd lost to the Archers whilst betting from the office yesterday. He'd backed favourite after favourite, and all had been beaten. He'd owed them a further £1,800 from before that, so it was essential he made a couple of grand tonight. He'd decided that unlike his mates he was a shrewd gambler. Everyone knew that shrewdies don't bet big on every race, so Dan thought he'd limit his bets to £200 pounds per race for interest until his big fancy of the night ran in the 8.47. He vowed to back the dog to win whatever sum of money he owed the Archer Brothers.

Chasing losses sat comfortably with Dan. However, by the time of the 9th race that night at The Stow, the 8.47, Dan was feeling decidedly uneasy, not to mention drunk, as he and his friends had consumed a pint of lager during each 15-minute interval between races. He'd only had small bets on the earlier races for interest's sake, but the fact was that it was already turning out to be a bad night. Eight losing bets of £200 meant £1,600 pounds lost on dogs he didn't particularly even fancy. Even worse, it meant that he owed the Archer Brothers £5,800, and he knew that he could expect their statement on Monday.

The only way out was to lump on Trap 3, the hot favourite in the 8.47.

Dan stood a few steps up in the stands overlooking the row

[27]

of bookmakers' pitches in front of him. This was an 'open' race, called such because the runners in the race came from other tracks around the country. Greyhounds are usually kennelled at their domestic track and run all their races there, unless they qualify for competitions, or races open to dogs from other tracks. Tonight's Trap 3 runner was from Hove, a track he'd visited shortly after leaving Lancing. Hove was not far from home, and he'd returned several times, surprisingly winning money on each occasion. He tried to reassure himself that this was a good omen.

Dan was going to have his biggest bet ever on the Hove dog in Trap 3. This was not down to his own strength of confidence in the selection, but out of a sense of necessity. If he was going to struggle paying the Archer Brothers' already substantial bill, he knew that they might refuse him further bets until the account was paid. He also knew that only by placing his wager with the Archers would he be accommodated for the size of bet he intended to have.

One of the bookies towards the end of the line, situated in front of where he stood, started chalking up prices on each of the six dogs. He was the first bookmaker to do so. Others quickly followed. Soon, with one surprise exception, every pitch was displaying prices. Trap 3 was a very short price at a general 8/11. With only a couple of minutes until 'the hare is running' announcement was to go over the tannoy system, Dan was beginning to panic. The lights dimmed, a sign that the race would begin imminently. He pushed past a couple of racegoers and marched straight up to Joss Archer and not without a degree of anger asked, "Why are you not showing prices?"

Joss took a drag from his Cuban cigar and grinned at Dan. He replied, "You're first in my queue son," and chuckled. Dan lost his temper at this point.

"You're the only sodding bookie I have credit with, and you don't want to lay a bet," he stormed.

At this Joss reached for a piece of chalk and by Trap 3 marked a dash, meaning even money. Dan was shocked. His anger dissipated and was replaced with a feeling of apprehension. Why would Joss want to lay this one dog at evens when all his rivals were odds-on?

As Dan was thinking, he was engulfed by a scrum of punters rushing in front of him with tenners and twenties, trying to avail themselves to the evens.

Joss Archer didn't want to lay any other dog in the race and was in full flow. "LAY EVENS THREE, LAY EVENS THIS GOOD THING!"

A man in a duffle coat and an east end accent shouted, "ERE JOSS, AN EVEN MONKEY?" meaning a bet of an even £500.

"AN EVEN MONKEY DOWN TO FRED. WHERE ARE YOU YUPPIES WHEN I NEED YOU?"

The moment had come. Dan pushed himself through the now-large throng around the Archer's pitch and stammered "Any chance of an even six grand, please Joss."

"AN EVEN SIX BAGS DOWN TO BOY," Joss shouted to

his brother Wayne, who was recording the bets as they streamed in. Wayne raised his eyebrows as he recorded the wager in the ledger.

Dan climbed back up the stairs of the stand, unsure whether to be proud or not that he'd just had a £6,000 bet without having even been given a ticket. The lights dimmed, the announcement "THE HARRRRE'S RUNNNING!" went out, and the six greyhounds sprang from the traps.

Trap 3 broke out in fourth place, was third around the first bend, and closing in on the leader around the penultimate bend, to the wild cheers of the delighted punters.

Dan couldn't bear to watch.

A few seconds later he knew his fate. The cheers of the crowd had turned to jeers. Having looked all over the winner around that penultimate bend, the favourite in Trap 3 had collided with another dog around the final bend, lost his momentum, and finished a close second.

One of Dan's mates, aware of his friend's enormous loss, clapped him on the back, not just to commiserate but to suggest that the rest of them were going for a curry and he should join them.

Curry was the last thing Dan wanted. He walked with his friend to the outside of the stadium, and past Charlie Chan's to the car park where the mini cab was waiting and the rest of his band were gathered in a huddle, no doubt discussing Dan's catastrophic gambling problem. There was silence in the minicab in the short journey to the nearby Pride of Punjab curry restaurant. The friends got out of the car, and despite their protestations Dan asked the driver to take him home.

Toxic Options

Chapter Four

Potential new employees at Sinclair Bank had to follow a thorough process of interviews. These were initially conducted by the Personnel Department, which would later be known as Human Resources, situated on the top floor of the bank, and subsequently by the candidates' prospective line manager. Should the candidate emerge successfully through those first two meetings, it was usual practice for other senior members of the department to conduct further interviews on a slightly less formal basis. Candidates that showed exceptional insight towards the financial markets and a personality to match, would be referred to one final meeting with the head of trading before a final decision was reached regarding whether an offer of employment would be made.

The trading department at Sinclair Bank was not just limited to the large dealing room in Liverpool Street, as it also had a large presence on the floor of the London Stock Exchange. To the side of the main trading floor where brokers and jobbers plied their trade, was the London Traded Options Market. This was comprised of what were known as options traders; traders similar to Dan and his peers, but who specialised in the trading of financial 'bets' that forecast where a share price might be in a specified amount of time. The Traded Options Market had been formed in the early 1980's, and within a short time was trading in huge daily volumes. Speculators could buy or sell at a fraction of the price of the underlying shares.

The prices of these options fluctuated violently, and the

potential for huge gains or losses was an ever-present concern for the risk committees at the world's banks. Only the previous year a scandal had led to the demise of one of Sinclair's rivals. Barings had been a London-based merchant bank that was established in 1762, which collapsed after suffering losses of £827 million. These losses were the result of poor speculative investments in futures and traded option contracts executed by their employee Nick Leeson from the trading floor in Singapore. Risk management had suddenly become an extremely important business, the banks desperately wary about the same type of disaster ever befalling them.

Whilst Dan was not one of the option traders on the floor itself, he did have a certain amount of influence on the positions that Sinclair Bank's floor traders entered into, and it was part of his job to monitor the size and risk of the positions involved. If concerned, he was required to inform the head of trading and the bank's risk committee. Dan would visit the floor on a daily basis, walking down to the Stock Exchange in Throgmorton Avenue and staying for about twenty or thirty minutes, during which he'd discuss with each of the Bank's traders their outlook on the future direction of share prices and markets in general, as well as some personal interactions. He had a good relationship with them, and their respect, as he was regarded as a wise head on young shoulders, at least when it came trading in stocks and options.

The morning after his disastrous loss, Dan was trying to peruse a number of CVs that had landed on his desk from Personnel. However, his mind was not focused so much on the documents in front of him. Instead, he was thinking about what he was going to do when the Archer's account arrived.

Despite his responsibilities at the bank, he felt he wasn't paid a great deal of money, just £40,000 per annum plus a reasonable bonus at year's end, though that was well over treble his salary from when he'd joined the bank as a teaboy a few years earlier. With the extortionate rent that he paid for his Fulham flat and his insatiable desire to gamble, he hadn't saved any money despite working for nearly eight years. His father had bailed him out so many times, but had told him in no uncertain terms that there would not be a next time. £11,800 owed to the Archer brothers was going to take a deal of finding.

As he continued examining the CVs, most of which he'd discarded, he noticed the photograph of a very pretty girl alongside the name *CIARA ROGERS*. She had striking looks, he thought, dark shoulder length hair, defined cheekbones, and the barest hint of a smile.

"She's alright, definitely alright," he mused. He read the profile under the girl's contact details, aware that the devil was in the detail, not the photograph. The looks were merely a bonus.

An ambitious graduate with a first degree in applied mathematics from Trinity College Dublin and internships with Allied Irish Bank and Société Générale, seeks employment at ground level with leading UK Bank.

"Well Ciara," he mused. "Today may be your lucky day." He

cast aside the other CVs and put hers in a drawer in his desk. Ciara was going to get an interview. Dan rose from his chair, put his suit jacket on, and made his way out of the office to visit his team of traders on the stock exchange floor.

The floor of the exchange was unusually busy that day. Better than expected figures from British Telecom had been posted, and there was takeover speculation surrounding General Electric Company. Prices across the electrical sector were in orbit.

Dan studied his trader's positions and nodded his approval, but he suggested trimming part of a position here and increasing a position there. He noted that they still owned an unusually large bull position in Standard Electric, which was fortuitous as the stock had risen steadily since the position had been acquired.

The electrical sector trader responsible for the position was a fellow Dan had personally recommended to the management at Sinclair Bank, and had been with the bank for just a few months. He'd previously worked for a rival firm on the floor. He was an Irishman named Mark O'Brien, and was two years older than Dan. He had dark curly hair, was thick set and quietly spoken, with a strong Irish accent. Dan wondered what Mark thought of him, what he thought about Dan being his senior despite having less experience, not to mention being paid considerably more. They appeared to have an amicable relationship however, without necessarily counting each other as great friends.

It was with this in mind that Dan was surprised when Mark asked if the two of them could have lunch together. Dan had no other plans for lunch that day, and agreed, albeit curious to know what was on Mark's mind. It was past midday and there were several restaurants in Throgmorton Avenue, all habitually frequented by stockbrokers and stockjobbers. They had chosen the Long Room Bar and Grill. Whilst it was an almost exclusively male preserve due to the relatively small number of women employed on the floor of the exchange, it had a jovial atmosphere about it whilst being intimate enough to have a private conversation with one's lunch companion. Dan loved the place. He'd first had lunch here with his dad and Sir Marcus Holderness, by way of a celebration for him gaining his job at Sinclair Bank.

Dan and Mark O'Brien briefly regarded the menu, then ordered a pint of beer each, followed by steak and chips and a bottle of Côtes du Rhône.

Dan could wait no longer to find out the reason for this impromptu lunch. "Come on then matey, I know we're not down here to discuss Amstrad or General Electric. What's up?"

Mark downed the remnants of his pint, lit a cigarette, and subtly looked around to make sure nobody was eavesdropping on their conversation. He replied, speaking slowly and deliberately in a hushed tone, his Irish lilt like a horseracing trainer from that country might be having been whilst interviewed after winning a horse race.

"Listen Dan, it's well known that you like gambling, and, if you don't mind me saying, you have little or nothing to show for it, despite being one of the banks star traders."

Dan remembered the £11,800 he owed the Archer Brothers. He felt agitated, unsure of where this was going.

Mark continued, "The thing is, I have a friend, a friend that works in corporate finance at Wade Bank. He's told me that they're working on a takeover. The problem is, if you call this a problem, is that it's for one of the stocks I cover. Geneva Electric are going to bid for Standard Telecom. Announcement on Monday. Do you know where I'm coming from?" He looked intensely at Dan. "When we left the floor, Standard were trading £1.39. Geneva are going to pay £2.00 in cash, and the whole deal has been agreed by both parties. If you've got money troubles, and I hear that you have, this could be your way out."

Dan gulped. He had his own stockbroker but had only ever used that firm to buy public share offerings in new issues such as British Gas and British Telecom. Maybe this was the way out, but at what risk? Numbers had already started rolling around in Dan's head. How many lots did he need to buy? How much did he need to make to get those Archer brothers off his back?

The great thing about buying options was that you could gain greater exposure for smaller risk. He considered that if someone in the know gave him a tip for a horse at 10/1 right now he'd have £1,200 or £1,500 on it in a flash. This was different though. This was a certainty – a real one.

Mark was in full flow now. "Get onto your broker and tell

him to come into the Electricals crowd this afternoon and ask him to quote the September £1.40 calls in Standards. The other guys will probably offer to sell them at 15 but I'll call them lower by a bit, to say, 14. Then get your man to buy 50 lots. I'll sell them to your broker, and next week you sell them back and we'll share the profit. So long as your guy keeps his mouth shut who he's dealing on behalf of it's safe as houses.

"It's not like we're defrauding Sinclair's anyway. As you saw earlier, I've been buying call options in these for weeks so the bank won't lose out. In fact, the bank will also clean up, and when the announcement that the bid is agreed at £2 per share, our calls will be worth 60p, us having paid 14p.That's a profit of 46p times £500 per point. Twenty-three grand between us. Even better, you won't even have to pay up front for them, as we'll trade out of our position as soon as the announcement comes out."

Dan considered his options. Insider dealing was not something he'd contemplated before, but the chances of getting caught were negligible. He knew that this practice was rife on the floor and had only been outlawed a few years earlier – it was even still legal in Holland.

Yes, he thought. *Everyone else is at it, why not me?*

"You're a bad man Mark, but count me in," he said.

Toxic Options

Chapter Five

She certainly looked the part. She'd bought an expensive Armani suit, with money lent to her by her parents, and had taken a considerable amount of time that morning making herself look like the professional that she expected to become. Whilst nervous inside, she appeared more like an experienced barrister interviewing for a role at a new chamber than the graduate intern that she really was.

Ciara had taken the tube to Liverpool Street, and as she emerged, she saw that she was over an hour early for her interview. She'd planned this deliberately, as she wanted to get as close as she could to the Sinclair Bank building and catch up with all the latest financial news as quickly as possible.

She found a branch of WHSmith's, a large newsagent, within the concourse of the train station at Liverpool Street and bought a copy of *The Financial Times* before walking into a café. She ordered a black coffee, found a table, and put her handbag aside. She glanced at the headline of the newspaper.

GENEVA ELECTRIC EXPECTED TO ANNOUNCE TAKEOVER OF STANDARD TELECOM.

She digested the headline article and turned to the markets column of the paper to catch up on the current levels of the FTSE, Wall Street, and Far Eastern markets. She noted the price of sterling and the dollar, and then turned to the back page where she read the

[41]

widely acclaimed commentary of the day's most important financial news in the 'Lex' column.

The title of the comment read *GE BID BETTER THAN STANDARD FOR TELECOM SHAREHOLDERS.*

It continued: *It is reported in this paper today that an agreed takeover of Standard Telecom by electrical giant Geneva Telecom has been agreed by both parties. It is likely to be announced on the London Stock Exchange as early as this morning. If the reported price of the offer of £2 per share is accurate, it will prove to be a huge tonic for long suffering shareholders of Standard Telecom.*

Standard's shareholders would have no doubt been delighted with an offer of only half that price under a year ago. It was merely last October that the company reported dire revenue and earnings together with a warning that trading conditions remained difficult, culminating in the share price reaching a three year low of 78p.

The current offer if accurate however, does not underestimate the net worth of Standard, who have undergone a transformation since the appointment of David Haine as Chief Executive at the turn of the year. His shareholders should be grateful at the fine job he has done, if not frustrated that £2 per share may not reflect the true future worth had Haine been left without the attentions of a predator as mighty as Geneva.

The official announcement had come out in pre-trading hours on Reuters. Dan Perry had seen it the moment he turned his screens on at

7.30 am. He'd punched the air with delight and shouted "OI OI OI!" to the slight bemusement of some of the analysts already in the office a few rows down from his desk.

One turned to his immediate colleague and joked "Dan's clearly had a winning bet on the Japanese golf." Little did they know that he'd made £11,500, trading on the breaking story of the day, let alone the means by which he'd achieved it.

Ciara entered through the slide open doors of Sinclair Bank and approached the reception desk.

"Ciara Rogers for an 11 o'clock meeting with Mr Dan Perry, please," she said.

The elderly receptionist checked his clipboard to view the appointment list and picked up the telephone to dial. A minute later he replied "Aye, luv, Mr Perry will be down shortly. Please take a seat."

Ciara smoothed her skirt down and took a seat in reception. Shortly afterwards a well-dressed young man with a very broad smile extended his hand to her.

"Dan Perry," he beamed. "Welcome to Sinclair Bank."

Dan was not usually the easiest of interviewers, but that day he was charm personified. He'd earlier written out a cheque to Archer Brothers Bookmakers for £11,800, but aside from the fact that he'd finally got the bookmakers off his back, at least until the next time his gambling racked up a large sum in losses, he felt a huge weight had been lifted from his shoulders. Not only had he and Mark O'Brien made a killing, so had the firm, and he knew that from the day's events only good could come career wise for both him and Mark.

"Now tell me Ciara, why do you really want to join this ghastly profession?" he asked.

"Well, I have a degree in applied mathematics and a massive interest in all financial markets. If I could combine the two and work in traded options, it would be my perfect job, especially at an institution as prestigious as Sinclair Bank," was the well-rehearsed reply.

Dan liked her, not just for her obvious intellect but from a purely male perspective. He struggled to distract himself from staring at her nyloned legs and perfect cleavage. The photograph on her resume didn't do her justice. He didn't have a girlfriend at the moment and thought to himself, "you never know."

The interview lasted for about an hour. If anything, Dan was being interviewed by Ciara before the end. She asked questions about every single aspect of the business, many of which Dan had to bluff his way out of as he didn't really know. He certainly wanted to impress her as much as she wanted to impress him back. The truth was that he'd probably already decided in reception that she was going to be working on his team.

As the process drew to a close, he had an idea. He'd badly wanted to speak to Mark all day, but last Friday they'd agreed not to talk on Monday, assuming matters had turned out as Mark expected.

All Sinclair Banks telephone lines were recorded, and it was not worth taking undue risk. One word out of place heard by hostile investigators was not an option. He shuddered at the consequences of something going wrong. A lengthy enquiry? Court? Prison? Disgrace!

"Ok Ciara, I like what I've heard," he said. Ciara was young and inexperienced, but Dan thought there would be little risk in the bank hiring her as a 'blue button', the most junior of the trading ranks.

"I think that you may make a decent blue button on our floor trading team," he continued. "But I'll need to introduce you to the guys down there before we can proceed further. We'll take a walk down to the Stock Exchange, and I'll introduce you to some of the team."

Ciara accepted readily, and twenty minutes later Dan and Ciara walked onto the floor of the exchange. Today was a quiet one, more subdued than by normal standards, but with one gaping exception. There must have been over a hundred people in the electrical sector. Brokers were screaming requests for prices in both Standard Telecom and Geneva Electric, as they had been since the opening bell.

Mark saw them standing at the edge of the crowd expectantly, but they seemed unwilling to distract him from trading, and kept their distance as they watched the action from beyond. He waved at them and smiled. Then he looked again, paying rather more scrutiny to the attractive dark-haired girl wearing a visitor's badge at Dan's side. His smile vanished at once. He cursed under his breath.

"Well, well, well Ciara Rogers as I live and breathe," he said jovially, approaching them. "What in God's name are you doing here?"

Dan thought Mark seemed somewhat uneasy in Ciara's company and asked how they knew each other. Ciara explained that they'd known each other when children in Dublin.

"I'm trying to persuade Dan here to give me your job," she joked.

Dan decided that this was not the ideal opportunity to have a discussion with Mark about their illicit gains, and left Ciara with him whilst he went to examine his other traders' positions. He resolved to leave Ciara with Mark to let her observe him trading for another half an hour or so, then introduce her to a few of the others before sending her on home. As far as he was concerned, subject to dealing with the personnel department, Ciara Rogers was Sinclair Bank's new blue button. He'd need to ask Mark about her before he placed them together in the electricals crowd, however.

When Dan had finished commenting on his other traders' positions and advised them on forthcoming trading strategy, he walked back to the electricals pitch. Somewhat to his annoyance, there was no sign of either Mark or Ciara. He asked an old colleague, now trading electrical options for Hoare Govett, if he'd seen them only to be told that they'd left the floor half an hour earlier.

It was after 1.00 pm now. Dan returned to his office, planning to call Mark after trading on one of the bank's telephones to suggest meeting for a drink after work. He knew that he'd bought 50 of the September 140 calls on Friday, as by prearrangement he'd called his broker on his mobile phone on Saturday and had it confirmed.

"Bought you 50 at 14 Dan. Your bank sold them to me," the broker had said. However, Dan still wanted confirmation that the sale side of the trade had gone through that morning though.

He had another idea. If Mark had gone temporarily AWOL, he'd find the broker himself.

He left the floor and went to one of the payphones, whose calls he knew were not recorded, located near the entrance to the floor, and dialled the number of Edwin James and Co. He was told that his broker was currently executing an order and might be found on one of the equity jobbers, Pinchin Denny's, oils pitch.

Dan found him within a minute. The broker was in his forties, definitely not a public-school type, but had worked in the market all his career and could spot the difference between a coincidence and a dodgy trade in his sleep. The broker winked at Dan.

"You old bastard!" he said jovially. "Sold your 50 lots at 60p. Drinks on you, son. Hope you don't get into the shit though."

Dan shuddered and returned to the office. Surely he'd be ok? Twenty-three grand was nothing, after all. It was the bigtime crooks the authorities were interested in.

When back at his desk, he called Mark again. Still no reply. After several more attempts he called one of the lads in the retail sector that he'd earlier advised on trading strategy, only to hear that Mark hadn't been spotted all afternoon. He called the Long Room Bar and Grill in case Mark had taken Ciara to what would have been by then, an extremely long lunch, but again to no avail.

At 6pm, feeling exasperated, and slightly nervous that something maybe wasn't right, Dan finally switched his screens off, left the office, and headed home.

Chapter Six

Late November 1986

Sir Marcus was in a quandary. Realistically, he knew that he should avoid speaking to Dan Perry altogether and report him directly to the Securities and Futures Association for further investigation. That would entail Dan being summoned to the Security and Futures Authority Offices on Queen Victoria Street for an intense taped interview in front of SFA officials and a detective from the Serious Fraud Office of the Metropolitan Police. On the other hand, he liked the boy, and had enjoyed a career long friendship with his father.

To be fair, the £23,000 that Dan had made was towards the lower end of the scale. All the names on Marcus's list were market professionals who worked under the scrutiny of the Securities and Futures Association, and he knew that profits of £50,000 or more were automatically reported to Queen Victoria Street.

Marcus' lunch with Dan's father, Brian Perry, had been only the week before, and he still hadn't said anything about the matter to the man. He wanted more time to consider his options. He wondered if it was ethical of him to warn Dan that he may be in a great deal of trouble. After all, the offence of insider dealing, if convicted, carried an unlimited fine and a maximum jail sentence of seven years.

Marcus noted down five of the names on the offenders list, those that had made varying profits of between £50,000 and £175,000 on the Geneva Electric takeover of Standard Telecom. Then he picked up the phone and asked his secretary to furnish the Securities and Futures Authority with the five names.

The remaining names, including Dan's, would be placed on a watch list and be monitored constantly in the future for any other instances of insider dealing. Perhaps this was an impending disaster that might be averted? It was with this in mind that he asked the secretary to contact Hamdan.

Hamdan was the elderly superintendent that presided over the waiters on the stock market floor. The waiters were responsible for assisting any of the dealers on the floor, on anything from organising the delivery of newspapers, mending broken telephones, and general security within the stock exchange building.

He put down the phone. It wasn't often that Sir Marcus Holderness's secretary called him, so it must be something important, he mused to himself. She'd asked him to find Dan Perry from Sinclair Bank, and requested that Hamdan should ask him to visit the twenty-third floor and ask for Sir Marcus Holderness, who wanted to have a "brief conversation" about "a certain matter". In Hamdan's long experience as a waiter he knew that to be summoned to the twenty-third floor was usually a sign that someone was in trouble.

He spotted the lad on the side of the electricals crowd, talking to the pretty Irish girl, Ciara.

Ciara was gorgeous, thought Hamdan. Nice with it too, unlike some of the stuffy old stockbrokers who looked down their nose at him.

He walked over to Dan and respectfully ventured, "May I have a word with you, sir? In private," whilst smiling bashfully at Ciara.

Hamdan and Dan walked the few yards to the entrance of the floor, where the head waiter was situated throughout the floor trading hours of the working day.

"Sir," he began quietly. "I have been asked to inform you that Sir Marcus Holderness has made a request that you visit him in his office on the twenty-third floor at some stage this morning. You will need to take the lift up, and the receptionist will be expecting you."

Dan reacted exactly as Hamdan expected, the way they always reacted. He'd seen the same expression each time he'd performed this unenviable task over the past twenty or so years that he'd been head waiter. They always did the same thing. They'd frown and look utterly indignant. They'd say "What, me? Are you quite sure?" as all semblance of colour drained from their faces.

Sadly, he thought, this was no different. Another ruined career. Hamdan watched as Dan walked slowly off the trading floor and turned the corner towards the lifts and the unenviable climb to the dreaded twenty-third floor.

The march of the condemned man.

"I have a meeting with Sir Marcus," Dan said confidently to the receptionist. He feared what the topic of conversation was to be about. He was quaking inside, a feeling he'd never experienced when due to meet anyone, least of all his father's close friend, but knew he needed to start acting, and acting well.

Confidence, he thought. *Confidence without arrogance.*

The receptionist led him down a long corridor and knocked on the door.

"Come in," said Sir Marcus. "Thank you, Jane."

Dan found himself in Sir Marcus's office, an office that he'd never seen the likes of. It was more like the living room of a very wealthy man. Deep pile carpet, four comfortable and expensive looking sofas, with oil paintings on each wall.

Sir Marcus smiled at him kindly and clasped his hands together, not offering to shake Dan's hand. "Dan my boy, how nice to see you again. How are things?" he asked, beckoning him to take a seat in front of his large mahogany desk. "I had lunch with your dad only last week."

Dan, determined not to show how fast his heart was pumping, routinely replied that things were going well at Sinclair Bank, that he'd recently been promoted again, and asked politely about Marcus's wife, Diana. He wished that Marcus would get to the point.

Perhaps he was wrong? Maybe this was to do with some forthcoming social occasion?

[52]

As if.

"Dan, I'll come straight to the point. I'm most concerned about you," said Sir Marcus. He paused and let his spectacles run down his nose as he viewed the list of names in front of him.

Dan felt sick.

Marcus continued, "I have in front of me a list. As you will no doubt be aware, my position within the Stock Exchange is Head of Regulation and Compliance. From time to time I am sent, by members of my department, lists of people who have fallen under our scrutiny. It's our collective responsibility here to spot suspicious dealing activity." He had deliberately decided not to be specific by mentioning the Geneva Electric/Standard Telecoms deal. He wanted to see Dan's reaction.

"Unfortunately, Dan, your name is on one of these lists which concerns suspicious dealing activity. Now, I must tell you that I have not, and will not, mention this to your dad, but I would advise you to possibly tell him yourself. I don't want to frighten you in any way, but I've seen how these situations can develop, and it can become expensive legally to defend oneself if things manifest in the wrong way, not to mention the severity of the consequences if found guilty.

"Someone in my department has been monitoring your personal trading activity recently, and frankly, it doesn't look very good. I'm not going to be any more specific than that at this point, but I will say this: whatever you have done or are thinking of doing again, you must stop it right now. Furthermore, I have the names of others at your bank on this list. I strongly suggest that you speak to them in private."

Dan's world had just turned upside down. He hadn't quite expected this. He'd guessed that he was in trouble, there had been little doubt about that, but Marcus hadn't mentioned the others on his list. He wondered if Mark O'Brien's name was there, but had no idea who the others from Sinclair Bank were. He thought wryly for a split second that those creepy analysts that sat in front of him in the office, with their Oxbridge degrees and Hermès ties, had probably been involved too, but how would they have known? He felt bewildered, lost. Like being back at school facing the headmaster.

"Well, Marcus, to be honest I'm completely shell shocked," said Dan. He had to make the best out of what was now a very bad situation. "I must confess that I made a few quid out of buying some options in Standard Telecom before the takeover, but I certainly had no inside information, assuming that's what you're implying. It was an innocent but highly fortunate punt, no more, no less."

Dan felt his self-confidence rising, despite his lies. Telling a tiny part of the truth surely made him more believable than an outright lie? "And who exactly would you like me to speak to about this?" he continued, with just a hint of aggression.

Sir Marcus noticed sarcasm in Dan's tone. He replied calmly, "Dan, I've been a close friend of your father for many a year now, and I'm incredibly embarrassed that I find myself in this situation with you. You're a top chap and I'm delighted to hear how well your career is going, although slightly concerned that your dad tells me that he's worried you have a gambling problem.

"That's none of my business though. This is. This insider dealing thing will most probably come to nothing, but I am already breaching my professional standards by even having this conversation with you. The fact is that you had never bought any traded options for your personal account in any company before Standard Telecom. Perhaps it's unfortunate that the first time you've traded in options, it was in them. Perhaps not.

"Furthermore, it's unfortunate that when my team questioned your stockbroker at Edwin James and co. about it, he said that the trade was affected at a cheaper price than was available from the other market makers by your own dealer at Sinclair Bank, something that our records had already confirmed.

"If you've done nothing wrong, I'm sure you won't hear of the matter again. I'm just warning you to be extremely careful going forward as next time, if there is a next time, I won't be able to prejudice my position by speaking to you first. By that I mean if we need to take things any further.

"Now off you go, and regards to your father." After a brief pause, Marcus corrected himself. "Actually, forget that. It might be better, ahem, for him not to know we had this conversation, despite my earlier advice, but I'll leave that decision up to you."

The entire conversation had lasted less than fifteen minutes.

In the lift back down to the floor, Dan's mind was working in overdrive. What had Marcus meant when he said, "If the situation develops the wrong way"? "How things can manifest", and the talk of legal fees for a potential defence had him on edge.

On the other hand, he recognised that his father's friend had been trying to help him and was partially comforted to recall him saying that things probably wouldn't go any further. He'd just have to wait, and to pray it would be true.

Hamdan spotted him as he walked from the lifts. The young man didn't return to the trading floor. They rarely did.

Chapter Seven

December 1986

Tower Bridge was not only one of the most recognisable bridges in the world, but it also provided a unique venue for corporate events and weddings. Overlooking the River Thames with stunning views of the metropolis, it housed three stunning venue areas, each one a unique setting for celebrations of every kind. The panoramic high-level walkways and the majestic Victorian Engine Rooms were in high demand that Christmas, offering the perfect venue for office parties, and that year it was the chosen location of the Sinclair Bank Trading department.

Much to Dan's chagrin, a memo had been sent to everyone in the department the previous month informing staff of the location and time of the party, with a sinister warning at the bottom saying *ATTENDANCE IS MANDATORY*. The previous year, the bank had hired a huge function room at the Dorchester Hotel only to find that the event was somewhat undersubscribed by a large portion of the seventy-strong trading department. These occasions were not inexpensive, and aside from the grand room being sparsely occupied by the members of staff that had attended, a great deal of fine food, beer, wine, and champagne had gone to waste, although the directors of the bank had kept the drinks on the premise that they would be stored within the bank for the purposes of 'client entertainment'.

One of the absentees had been Dan, who was of the opinion that he should be entitled to party and drink with his own friends, in his own time, rather than spend a dreary evening talking to the directors, settlements staff, or anyone else that he generally disliked amongst his colleagues.

He'd also heard a rumour that the Compliance Officer had been invited this year. As far as Dan knew, the compliance department would not have been made aware of his little indiscretion earlier in the year. He still hadn't heard anything back since his meeting with Sir Marcus, which he considered good news, but he really didn't want to be making polite conversation with a man who evidently took great pleasure in catching members of staff breaking Stock Exchange rules, such as himself.

Even worse was the fact that they had to wear black tie, which meant a tedious visit to Moss Bros., the formal attire outfitters, after work. Or worse, he could have to go on a Saturday. Dan considered this to be time misspent, when he could have been drinking or reading the form for the day's racing instead.

Dan looked at himself in the mirror of the Sinclair Bank men's lavatory on the second floor as he adjusted his bowtie. He'd lost his elasticated one and was disappointed that they only had the kind you had to tie yourself in Moss Bros.

He looked at his watch. 6.15pm. He'd arranged to meet some of his peers in The Crispin, the pub around the corner in Broadgate, where he played shoot pool on Friday nights for large amounts of money. Today being a Friday, he knew that his gambling pals, most of

[58]

whom were traders from rival banks, would be there as usual and expecting him to play. Tonight, however, he thought he'd probably be best to leave it and socialise with his Sinclair Bank peers.

nightmare.   Yes, he thought. *Just a few pints then off to the Tower Bridge*

It was 6.30 when he entered the pub, which was as packed as it was every Friday evening. The first person he saw whom he recognised was Mark O'Brien, buying a round of drinks. Ciara was there too, with a dozen or so other traders both from the floor and the office.

Dan had found himself increasingly thinking about Ciara recently. She could have fronted any television advert or magazine cover, but she had a natural beauty that Dan felt was more attractive than the look of a photo-shopped model. There was something about her, a shyness and hesitation in her body movements and a softness in her soft Irish lilt. Her cream dress had a tailored look that was bold against her short, dark hair. She was strikingly tall too, and in her heels was considerably taller than Dan's six foot. He pictured her in stockings and suspenders with her legs astride him.

Standing just a few feet away from her, he realised at that moment he was hooked. He had considered asking her out for dinner, but this would no doubt have got out and been embarrassing for him professionally. And even worse, what if she said no?

He was curious about her relationship with Mark too. Was it strictly professional, or was there another element to their relationship? They'd clearly known each other from before their Sinclair Bank days. Dan cursed himself for having placed her in the electricals crowd on the floor as Mark's blue button. It was something he'd address in the new year, he decided. She could be transferred to the stores sector. He'd call it 'widening her horizons.'

"What yer drinkin' Guv?" shouted the dinner-jacketed Mark, spotting his boss. Dan requested a pint of lager and moved over to the group. They talked about the party, the Tower Bridge location, and what time they could leave without getting in trouble with their bosses.

Dan was in earnest conversation with one of his colleagues about the future direction of Wall Street when he noticed one of his Friday night gambling pals at the bar looking in his direction. Dan excused himself and scrambled through the Friday night throng to his friend, whereupon another pint of lager was handed to him.

"We're in the far corner over there," the friend said. Dan looked over to see another four of his usual Friday night crowd in the far corner of the pub looking impatient to start the dealing again as they awaited their next round of drinks. Dan secretly wished that he was with them, but explained that tonight was the night of the Sinclair Bank Christmas party and that with his colleagues there he'd best duck out of the proceedings that night.

"Come on matey, you lost your bottle?"

"OK just a couple of rounds, and I want to be banker for one of them," said Dan, walking over to the corner of the pub. Shoot pool is a very simple, but highly dangerous game. It involves seven £1 coins being stacked on top of each other by the 'banker', which is a role that each player in the group has a turn as. The chosen banker then specifies a 'pot'; a sum of money that he is prepared to lose. The lads Dan played with usually had pots of £50, typically increasing as the evening went on. The banker will then turn to the player on his immediate left, who is required to predict heads or tails and the sum he wishes to bet on the outcome. The player may only stake up to the amount in the pot. Should the player win, the value of his win is deducted from the pot, and should he lose that sum is added to the pot instead. Then it is time to turn the next coin, and the next player has a chance to call. The round ends either when the sum of the banker's pot has reached zero, thereby the banker having to pay out the full stake of his original pot, or when the last remaining player has had his call, whichever outcome comes first. At any time in the round a player may 'shoot for the pot'. That means he can back heads or tails for everything that's remaining. Whilst the banker can never lose more than the size of the original pot, in this case fifty pounds, several losing calls by the players can push the size of the pot up considerably. Once the round is finished, the banker retains all the money, if any, left in the pot.

Dan took his seat at the table and placed his pint down. "Right lads," he said. "I'm only staying for two rounds, and I'll be banker for one of them. You know I'd prefer to stay here all night rather than go to this stupid party, but that's life."

No one seemed to mind. He reached for the seven £1 coins in

the middle of the table, shuffled them in his hands and made a neat stack of them in front of him.

"There's a hundred quid in the pot, gentlemen," he said.

At 7.30pm, after ten rounds, they had been playing for an hour. As was entirely usual, the stakes had increased as more beer was consumed. Dan had been losing. Having started as banker and promptly losing his first hundred pounds, he'd decided to quickly get his money back and shoot for the pot whenever the bank was up to high stakes. Shortly before he'd reluctantly had to retire and head for Tower Bridge, he'd found himself £800 down, having shot for a pot of £100, another for £150, and on his final round a tasty £450.

If only he'd stuck to just the two rounds that he'd planned on playing. Disgusted with himself, he reached for his cheque book and wrote several cheques to the friends that he'd lost to before making his excuses and leaving.

Back in the main part of the bar he was further annoyed to see that none of his Sinclair Bank colleagues had waited for him. He cursed himself for losing so much at that ridiculous game when he should have been showing off in front of Ciara.

Alone in the cab he decided to keep a very close eye on Mark and Ciara. He'd recently asked Mark if there was anything going on between them, which Mark had denied. Dan was not sure that he believed him, however, and decided to earnestly monitor the body language between them that night. If he could be convinced that they weren't shagging, he'd ask Ciara on a date after all.

The Friday night traffic ensured that the short distance between Broadgate and Tower Hill took rather longer than it should, and it was after 8pm that Dan found himself in the conference room within the bridge, by which time the party was in full flow. He accepted the glass of champagne that was proffered to him by a waiter as he entered the room before finding himself talking to a crowd of analysts discussing the oil prices.

"The US Dollar has been caught up in a price war orchestrated by Saudi Arabia, which will inevitably lead to the collapse of the US oil industry, triggering many years of production declines," one droned. Dan quickly made his excuses and moved on.

During the course of the next couple of hours he worked the room efficiently, ensuring that he spoke to all that he should, feigning interest and bonhomie, yet something was bugging him. Where were Ciara and Mark? All the other Sinclair staff that had been drinking earlier in the Crispin were present. He'd seen Mark and Ciara in their finery, so why on earth weren't they here? Ciara's absence especially was bound to be noticed, as men outnumbered the women at Sinclair Bank by about twenty to one.

"Dan, great to see you buddy," said the Compliance Officer, interrupting Dan's train of thought.

"Great to see you, Eddie," replied Dan, lying.

"Well, you guys have had another good year I see. How do you make so much money when one company takes over another?" Eddie asked.

"I suppose that's why you're in compliance and why we're traders, you asking questions like that," joked Dan, somewhat nervously. He was keen to finish this conversation immediately. He didn't want to get into a discussion with this man about takeover bids.

He felt his bow tie coming loose and seized the opportunity to extricate himself, making his way to the men's toilet. Away from the noise of the party now, he relieved himself before setting himself to the arduous task of fixing his bowtie in front of the mirror. A few minutes later, bow tie situation saved, he looked at his watch. 10.30.

This wouldn't take too much longer, he thought. He'd leave at midnight and take a cab home.

As he shut the heavy door of the toilet behind him, he was surprised to hear that the level of noise emanating from the party further down the corridor was considerably reduced. In fact, approaching the room, he suddenly realised that there was actually no noise at all. He wondered if he'd gone the wrong way and was about to enter a different, empty room whilst the party continued elsewhere.

Dan dismissed the thought. He'd had a fair amount to drink, sure, but in no way was he drunk.

He stepped inside the room. It was most certainly the same one, but there was not a single person there. He noticed a number of broken glasses and food that had tipped onto the carpet. A woman's handbag lay on the floor. Dan was feeling distinctly uneasy. His seventy strong department of colleagues had vanished.

There must have been a fire scare and they'd been

evacuated, he thought. He knew that he needed to get out of there, and fast too. He turned back to the entrance, rushed through the door, and made for the stone staircase that led down to the street level. It was then that he heard a man shouting at him from a long way down the stairs.

"Dan, where the fuck are you?" screamed the unmistakeable Irish accent of Mark O'Brien. "There's a fucking bomb scare. Get down here!"

The explosion a few seconds later was enormous. It was as if a wall of orange flame had decided to engulf the conference room. The corridor disintegrated and windows shattered. Smoke and fire rushed into the corridor and up the staircase. Thousands of shards of glass and nails, the deadliest of combinations, rained down. The fire alarm, shrill and deafening, erupted into life.

The force of the blast had literally lifted Dan off his feet as he'd started his decent of the wide stone staircase, and he fell down about twenty steps. Feeling terror the likes of which he'd never experienced before, he just managed to pick himself up and run down the remaining steps. At the bottom of the staircase he collapsed, choking from the fumes of the smoke.

Then there was silence and nothing but darkness.

Toxic Options

Chapter Eight

Dan regained consciousness slowly. He clumsily tried to get to his feet, choking on the smoke that now engulfed Tower Bridge's entrance and the Victorian engine rooms at the bottom of the stairs.

Mark had managed to extricate himself from the carnage and take in a few breaths of the icy night air outside straight after the explosion, but returned less than a minute later after realising that there was no sign of Dan. He took another deep breath and burst back into the chaos, closely pursued by two policemen. Whilst barely able to see anything as the swirling, dense. black smoke took its toll, Mark and the constables took only seconds to locate the source of the groaning body.

Dan had fallen down again. He could hear his rescuers calling his name, but the asphyxiating nature of the fumes made shouting impossible. The best he could manage were some helpless moans.

They sufficed, as now upon him, the policemen took one of his arms each and pulled him to his feet whilst Mark lifted his legs. They stumbled awkwardly towards the entrance, carrying Dan to safety and an awaiting St John's ambulance.

Pandemonium raged outside. The police had cordoned off the road both sides of the bridge within twenty minutes of the telephone call that they had received at Bishopsgate Police Station. They had been used to receiving hoax bomb threats since the early

1970s, but there was no doubting the authenticity of this one. The Irish voice at the end of the line had used the appropriate code word when he spoke to the desk sergeant.

The paramedic did some routine checks for internal bleeding, head injury, blood circulation, and pulse. Dan's face and hands were mired in blood, but despite that and the smoke he'd inhaled, his rescue had been swift.

Lying on the stretcher, he was suddenly aware of Ciara peering down at him. He could tell that she'd been crying.

"How are you feeling Danny boy?" she asked, concerned.

Dan actually raised a smile. "I probably lost more blood playing shoot pool in the Crispin," he croaked.

"Something like this puts gambling and trading into perspective my love," she whispered.

"I think he's going to be just fine," the paramedic reassured her cheerily. "He'll most likely have an overnight stay at Guy's and a hospital breakfast, then he'll be fit to play again tomorrow."

Dan looked up at Ciara and managed a smile. "Maybe I'll make it to Newbury Races tomorrow after all."

Despite his words, the paramedic was still eager to get Dan to Guy's Hospital for an examination, and the following morning Dan awoke in a hospital bed. He felt a bit battered and bruised, and nurse had to give him some paracetamol for his headache, but otherwise he felt in good order.

His mind spun at the events of the previous evening. He called his parents, who had only learned of the bombing on the radio when his mother had tuned in to Radio Four in the early hours of the morning.

"Darling, we've been *so* worried about you. We saw it on the news, and I said to Dad that I thought your firm were having your party in Tower Bridge. We've had a sleepless night. We rang you at home countless times, but you didn't answer, and we – we were just in despair!"

"Look, I'm fine Mum. I'm in hospital, but there is no real damage – just some bruises. I'm allowed out of here in a couple of hours, and I'll tell you the full story later when I'm home." For now, he gave his parents a brief resume of the events and reassured them that his health was more or less ok.

After he hung up, a nurse entered the ward with a trolley laden with tea, coffee and the morning's copies of a few different newspapers. When asked, Dan asked for black coffee and was told somewhat disapprovingly that no, they did not have either *The Sporting Life* or the recently established *Racing Post*.

He settled for *The Mirror*, whose headline screamed *CHRISTMAS HORROR AS IRA BOMB CITY CHRISTMAS PARTY*.

The report followed: *Late last night, Christmas revellers from leading City Investment House Sinclair Bank, were evacuated from their office party at London's famous Tower Bridge following a coded warning from whom police believe to be the Provisional IRA.*

A massive explosion followed the evacuation, causing extensive damage to the bridge itself and maximum disruption in the local area, but there are not believed to be any fatalities. One member of Sinclair Bank's staff is understood to be undergoing treatment for minor injuries.

Police are interested in hearing from any witnesses who saw two men running directly from the scene of the bombing at around 7.30pm last night. Both are understood to have been around six feet tall, casually dressed, and wearing masks resembling the Prime Minister.

Dan was released from Guy's Hospital in the afternoon, too late for him to get to Newbury races. He hailed a taxi to take him back to his flat in Fulham. As he was fumbling in his pocket for a fiver to pay the driver, he found a piece of paper that he did not recognise, which turned out to be a note from Ciara.

Please call me Dan, to let me know how you are. I can visit you if you're still in that wretched hospital. Ciara.

She'd left her number at the bottom. He knew that she lived in Central London. An idea came into his mind, an opportunity to good to miss. He let himself into his flat and lit a cigarette, then picked up the phone and dialled the number.

"Hi Ciara, London's finest trader here, calling from home. They let me out at 2."

"Oh, Holy Jesus, thank God you're ok Dan. We've all been

worried sick."

"No, I'm fine, really. It was all a hell of a shock but I'm nothing worse than a bit sore. As I didn't have any lunch, I'll need a decent dinner, but there's no food in the house and I don't feel up to going out to play with the lads tonight. I know it's late notice, but how about dinner? I need to give you your end of year appraisal," he joked.

Relieved that he sounded ok, she played with him. "You're London's finest trader, eh?"

"Well, I wouldn't necessarily say I was London's *finest*, but I'd definitely be in the top one percent. And why, may I inquire, are you asking?"

"Because it's mighty flattering for a mere blue button to be asked on a date by such a star trader,' she replied. "Yes, I'd love to go to dinner with you."

Dan felt his spirits soar and he pumped his fist, as he did when he'd had a large winning bet or landed a coup illegally in a stock. He suggested that they meet at the Il Pontevecchio restaurant on The Old Brompton Road at eight o'clock.

After disconnecting the call, he turned on the television and tuned into Channel 4, that had just taken the TV Racing rights off ITV. They were covering racing from Newbury and Ayr, but for once he didn't feel like gambling. He soon switched off the television and fell into a deep sleep, dreaming of Ciara.

It had been snowing most of the day, but he got a taxi easily and found himself at the restaurant at 7.45pm, where he ordered a large gin and tonic, lit a cigarette, and planned his strategy.

Ciara appeared at 8pm on the dot. She appeared strikingly different to the Ciara he knew from work. She wore a brown mink coat and a black dress which complimented her Amazonian figure and decanter-shaped waist. She broke into a smile, her oyster-white teeth sending an electric surge down his spine. He wanted to kiss those calamine pink lips on the spot but resisted the urge and settled for a couple of kisses to the air around her cheeks, European style.

The snogging might happen later, he reflected as a waiter politely took her coat. They settled at a table and began to discuss the terrible events of the night before. Dan's first question had been to ask why she and Mark hadn't got to the party until so late.

"We met some of our opposition traders from the floor by the taxi rank at Broadgate after we left the Crispin and were persuaded to join them in the Corney and Barrow's in Broadgate Circle. We were having such good craic that we didn't realise what the time was."

Then he asked her about her relationship with Mark, and how they had got to know each other before Sinclair Bank. She explained that they'd gone around with the same gang in Ireland during their teens and discovered alcohol, pubs, and discos together.

"I didn't know him very well, but he was certainly one of the lads," said Ciara.

Dan asked how they got on working together.

"He's a bright man and a good teacher. He's taught me a lot about traded options."

"And that's as far as it goes?"

"Dan, I hope you're not suggesting…" Ciara showed a flicker of annoyance, but it made Dan feel extremely relieved. There was clearly nothing going on.

"How would you feel if I moved you to another sector, the stores perhaps?"

Ciara mulled this over for a few seconds. "I think that could be a good idea. A bit of a change wouldn't be a bad thing, so long as you're not doing it because you're jealous of Mark". She said this with a smile as she didn't want Dan to feel embarrassed.

"Nothing could be further from the truth," Dan lied.

With the home truths out of the way, they spent the rest of dinner finding out more about each other. They discussed brothers, sisters, parents. She spoke about her time at Trinity College in Dublin and her internships at Allied Irish Bank and Société Générale. Dan told her about his own life and how he'd originally got the job with Sinclair. He felt at total ease with her, and she listened intently to his every word. He didn't even mind telling her that he hadn't been to university, or that his father's friend, Sir Marcus Holderness, had effectively arranged for him to be hired without having even met him. Ciara complemented him, saying that university would have been irrelevant in Dan's case given his acumen as a trader, and he returned it by saying what amazing progress she had made in her first five months.

They'd been eating, drinking, and chatting earnestly for over two hours. Ciara declined to have a pudding, but Dan ordered tiramisu and suggested they should share it, a gesture that she thought was sweet despite only having a teaspoonful when it arrived. They'd ordered several brandies and coffees, and Dan was impressed by how much drink she could take. It was that time when all men got nervous; the time to get the next step out of the way. He decided to just come out with it.

"Do you fancy going on to a club?" he asked, then cursed himself. That hadn't been what he intended to say. Why hadn't he had the guts to suggest that they have a nightcap at his flat?

She made it easy for him. "I'm not a nightclub type of girl anymore. You could always show me where a star trader lives though."

Dan's flat was a short cab ride from the restaurant. They talked about the dinner they'd just had, small talk considering they both knew what was coming next. He undid the latch and turned on the lights to the flat.

"I'll just get some champagne from the kitchen," he said. "Show yourself around."

Ciara stepped into a large bright living room, instantly impressed by an imposing large bookcase, modern furniture and an even more modern looking television. She removed her fur coat whilst admiring some of the art that adorned the walls and lay it on a sofa.

A minute or so later Dan returned to the living room armed with two flutes and an open bottle but was surprised to see no sign of her.

Perhaps she'd gone to the loo? he mused. He extracted a record, Handel's Water Music, from its sleeve and placed it on the stereo system, before walking down the corridor to his bedroom.

And there she was, sitting on the bed in just a bra, panties, stockings, and black stilettos.

"I'm moist already, Dan."

Dan needed no further encouragement. He reached for her hand and gently pulled her to her feet, before embracing her with all the pent-up passion he'd felt for her over the past five months. Breathing in her perfume he felt the familiar adrenaline rush of sexual arousal.

His clothes virtually fell off. Ciara, the junior blue button in the electricals crowd, was the epitome of femininity in her lingerie, her tall slender figure with curves that inspired in him such an intense attraction that he felt almost dizzy.

He laid her across the bed, and she instinctively arched her back, inviting him to undo her bra. He eagerly complied. She slid her silk panties down her legs, and he admired her thick, neat pubic hair, as she admired his now rock-hard cock.

Their lips met. He pulled her closer by the waist whilst his tongue devoured her mouth. She wrapped her long, stockinged legs firmly around his thighs and groaned in pleasure as he delved deep inside. They sighed together in unison as he penetrated her. His strokes were slow and considerate, and there were moments that he'd ease off, drinking in her beauty as they flowed together in unison.

There seemed no requirement for elaborate sexual positioning, nor oral stimulation. Her gasps became shorter and louder, and her face contorted with ecstasy as she approached orgasm. Dan too was nearing climax, and with one final flurry of rapid pumping she screamed, and as he came long and hard inside her Ciara experienced the most excruciatingly exquisite orgasm of her life.

Chapter Nine

March 1987

Sir Marcus Holderness had bought a racehorse. It had been his wife Diana's idea after they had attended a race meeting one Saturday afternoon at Sandown Park. They had been down to the paddock after each race to see the horses coming back in and witnessed the beaming expressions on the faces of the winning connections. Knowing that they could comfortably afford to buy something decent, they had decided to go ahead and buy one of their own.

Marcus hadn't had an enormous interest in the sport before, but like so many others before him was now captivated. He'd started reading the racing pages of the newspapers each day, and soon realised that to have a horse likely to win at the highest level he would probably need to invest in a jumps horse. That way they could avoid having to compete with the world's richest tycoons and Arab oil Sheiks that mostly frequented the winners' enclosure at Royal Ascot on the Flat.

He'd seen a trainer, Captain Neville Taylor, interviewed on television one day having just trained a big race winner. Marcus knew Captain Taylor from their National Service days when they had both served at Catterick, although their career patterns had subsequently led them apart with Marcus going into the City and Taylor remaining in the army. He remembered the captain being always first on parade, a crack shot, and a stickler to detail, with a work ethic that drew the respect of both his peers and senior officers. Captain Neville Taylor was an all rounder, an achiever. Marcus painfully remembered stepping into the boxing ring with him one day and receiving two black eyes and a cut lip in a bout that was heavily one sided. Still, Marcus considered him the archetype officer and a gentleman. He liked the cut of this man's jib and had decided to call him to discuss his potential new purchase.

"I'm a hands-on trainer Marcus, and don't like my owners calling me up all the time – not even old colleagues," the captain said briskly. "You'll get one call per week, at a predesignated time on a Sunday morning, lasting no more than five minutes, and I'll expect you to answer. You'll be sent one letter each week outlining your horse's progress. Other than that, the only contact we'll have will be at the races or when we meet socially during the summer season."

Marcus admired the trainer's authority and self-confidence and told Diana that night that he had agreed to have his first racehorse with Captain Neville Taylor, at his Heath Farm Stables in Lambourn.

Captain Taylor, having asked Marcus how much he was looking to pay for the acquisition, subsequently travelled to a sale in Ireland, armed with the knowledge that he could go up to thirty thousand guineas in order to secure a horse with the breeding and potential to win a race at the prestigious Cheltenham festival, the mecca for all fans of Jump Racing and the pinnacle of the National Hunt year. Captain Taylor returned with a handsome four-year-old bay gelding by the name of Beacon Boy.

Beacon Boy had run in two bumpers in Ireland. Bumpers are flat races run under National Hunt jumps rules but are only eligible to horses that have not run previously under normal flat racing rules. He'd run with credit in both the Irish races, shaping with promise behind subsequent winners. Captain Taylor had over thirty years' experience as a racehorse trainer and felt that Beacon Boy would prove to be a better hurdler and an even better steeplechaser. He secured lot 42 for a sum of twenty-eight-thousand-five-hundred guineas at auction.

His judgement had been sound, as under his care and new owners Beacon Boy's progress had been remarkable. Marcus and Diana had enjoyed a thrilling January day at Plumpton, a racecourse situated under the Sussex downs, when Beacon Boy won his British debut effortlessly, making all the running to win in a two-mile novice's hurdle. This fete was quickly surpassed when he won the feature handicap hurdle at Sandown just three weeks later. As Sir Marcus, Lady Diana and Captain Taylor had stood in the Sandown winners enclosure, a journalist thrust a microphone into the trainer's face.

"That was a brilliant performance from a very promising horse Captain Taylor, where do you go next?" The journalists all knew better than to address him as Neville.

"What do you think, young man?" replied a brusque Captain Taylor, not the easiest of interviewees, before answering his own question. "All roads lead to Cheltenham now."

The big day finally came. Cheltenham of 1987, The National Hunt

Festival. Marcus had been counting down the days after the Sandown race, but the opening Tuesday was now upon them.

He and Diana had driven to the course from London, leaving early to avoid the inevitable traffic congestion. They parked the Bentley in the owners and trainers' car park before walking the few minutes to the great amphitheatre. They were early, still with over three hours until the first race and five hours until the reappearance of Beacon Boy. They had been invited to their trainer's box but, being their first time at Cheltenham, decided to walk around the different enclosures first, taking in the atmosphere.

It seemed that most racegoers that chilly March day had also decided on getting there early, as there appeared to be thousands already in attendance. They recognised those now-familiar racecourse smells of crushed grass, beer, cigars, and cigarette smoke. The scent of fast food wafted through the air, burgers, hot dogs, pork roasting on spits: the smells of a giant barbecue. Punters called out to them things like "Good luck today Jonjo," or "I fancy yours in the first, Stevie."

They'd seen jockeys coming into the racecourse, wearing suits and carrying their bags on their way to the weighing room. Their own jockey, a semi-toothless young man in his late twenties was called Jamie Davies. Davies, due to ride Beacon Boy later, was 'retained' by Captain Taylor, which meant that the captain had priority over any other trainers when claiming his jockey to ride.

Captain Taylor always insisted that his jockeys appeared in his box precisely forty-five minutes before lunch was served, wearing suits and ties, to meet his friends and other horse owners to answer their questions. The jockeys all knew that they would be on the wrong end of a bollocking should they not have left the box within five minutes of the guests sitting down for lunch.

Marcus and Diana walked across the lawn, the impressive stands to their left and the glorious sight of the Cotswolds, a light covering of snow illuminating them on an overcast day, like a scene on a Christmas card.

Bookmakers were already taking bets. Sir Marcus noticed two rather gauche types shouting out odds. One, with long blonde hair, was dressed in a white suit and sheepskin coat and smoked a large Cuban cigar. Marcus recognised him from Sandown, where he'd relieved him and his brother of £1,000 when Beacon Boy had been the subject of his £125 winning bet at 8/1. He also recognised the slogan: *YOU PLAY, ARCHER BROTHERS PAY!*

Then, somewhat to his consternation, Marcus heard the man cry out "OI, GUVNOR!" and made the mistake of looking around. He found himself looking squarely at Joss Archer.

"YOUR 'ORSE GONNA WIN TODAY, GUVNOR?" Joss yelled once he saw he had Marcus' attention.

Marcus wasn't often embarrassed, but felt himself redden, having attracted the attention of a number of punters around the Archer Brothers' pitch.

"I certainly hope so," he spluttered. "Perhaps I'll come down later to have another bet with you." Then he took Diana's hand and led her away.

"Fucking toffs," Joss said under his breath, smiling to his brother, Wayne.

Dan Perry and Mark O'Brien had taken the day off and travelled up to Cheltenham from Paddington on the train. Dan had asked Ciara to join them, but she'd declined his offer, annoying him slightly.

He'd asked her one evening the previous week in a smart London restaurant whilst they were being entertained by brokers hungry to get Sinclair Bank's business. Dan and Ciara had been an item ever since the evening after the ill-fated Christmas party. Some nights would be spent at Dan's flat and others at hers, but some were spent apart, too. Ciara had insisted to Dan that their relationship should be kept strictly secret – they hardly wanted everyone in the office, let alone the stock exchange floor gossiping about them.

Their whirlwind romance had not featured any arguments until they'd got home to Dan's flat that night.

"For the life of me I don't understand why you won't come to the races with me and Mark next week," he'd said, rounding on her. "What the fuck is it with you two? I'll bet you'd come if he wasn't going."

"You stupid bastard," Ciara raged in reply. "How fucking dare you still be intimating that there's something between us, you jealous prick! How many times have I told you that we just knew each other as kids back in Ireland?"

She'd stormed off then to return to her own flat, even having considered giving Dan back the extra set of keys he'd had made for her. The following day however, they'd quickly made up, with Dan venturing a grovelling apology and producing a large bunch of flowers when he arrived at her flat that evening.

Mark and Dan, having drunk a few on the train earlier and another couple of pints at the pub outside Cheltenham Station, were now set for a full-on afternoon of tumultuous inebriation and, in Dan's case, heavy gambling. With no box to go to, the Arkle Bar seemed the next best option. It was situated at the bottom of the viewing lawn, underneath the luxury boxes. They would try and ponce whatever invitations they could to more luxurious and less crowded surroundings should the chance manifest later in the day. Dan knew that Beacon Boy was running in the Novices Handicap Hurdle later, and had been told by his father the previous day that Sir Marcus and Diana were going to be at the races, entertained by their trainer, Captain Neville Taylor. He harboured hopes that they'd bump into Marcus and receive an invitation. Still, the Arkle Bar would do for now.

It was like a high-ceilinged farmyard barn inside, sparsely furnished with framed pictures of newspaper clippings demonstrating past heroes of Cheltenham's glorious history. Legends of the turf both equine and human looked down on the huge throng of punters within. Paraffin burning stoves strategically adorned the floor keeping out the frosty weather outside, and long wooden ledges surrounded the walls and pillars as a resting place for scarves, papers and drinks.

Any amount of Champagne gin, vodka, whisky and sloe gin

would be consumed that week, but the bestseller by a distance was Guinness, the favoured tipple of the Irish.

With two hours to go before the first race the bar was packed and rocking with English and Irish punters both young and old, affluent and poor, loud laughter ringing out as they all drank in the atmosphere of Cheltenham's magic and the anticipation of the high-quality sport to come.

Near the front of the crowded bar, he thought about Ciara. She'd be trading on the floor right now, missing the fun and excitement of all this. Obviously, she'd been right; there couldn't be any connection with Mark, could there? After all, Mark had become one of his mates ever since the killing in the shares they'd made last year. They often drank together.

No, he wouldn't lie to me, mused Dan. He thought that maybe she cared for him so much that she didn't want to encourage him to gamble by going to Cheltenham. His debts had again started racking up a bit, and she'd recently noticed the Archer Brothers' statement lying open on a table in his flat. That bill for 37,500 had taken some explaining.

Captain Neville Taylor's box was high up in the main stand with a breath-taking view from the balcony. His guests were a mix of old friends built up over a lifetime, and a few select horse owners. They would enjoy smoked salmon and prawns followed by medallions of beef and new potatoes, all washed down with copious amounts of

Chablis and Chateauneuf du Pape. Various racing celebrities, including a few other trainers would be asked to join the guests after lunch for a drink or two in passing.

"Hand me that bottle, young man," Captain Taylor said to the waiter. He took the open bottle of champagne from the waiter's hand and started pouring the bubbles into two flutes, handing them to Sir Marcus and Diana.

"Not bad to have a runner at Cheltenham in your first season as an owner old boy," he said. "And a fancied one at that. I hope you're going to have a decent bet. I saw Beacon Boy was about 4/1 earlier."

"Our horse, Neville, and as yet I haven't had a bet," replied Marcus, winking at his trainer. Diana smiled gracefully in approval, as Beacon Boy was in both their names as owners.

"Damned rude of me. Forgive your trainer's oversight, please, Diana," ventured the captain before continuing. "Now, about that bet. Do you have an account with anyone down there?" He pointed down in the direction of the betting ring.

Marcus replied, "I don't, actually, but when we won at Sandown I did back him with that loud, long-haired fellow on the rails."

"Ha! With the long blonde hair, white suit, and wearing enough gold to sink a battleship?" ventured Captain Taylor.

Marcus smiled and nodded.

The captain continued, "Joss Archer and his brother Wayne. They're the biggest bookmakers on the rails in the South of England. Dogs and horses, and they usually offer the best prices. They may be wide boys, but they're ok.

"In fact, I like them enough to have an account with them. I may ask you to do something for me with them, after lunch. I'll give you my account number. They are used to my envoys placing bets on my behalf; I can't be seen betting on the rails. Bad for the image you know.

"Besides, I'll be saddling up Beacon Boy and giving that Davies lad tactical instructions so that we have the best chance possible of landing you your first festival winner and taking those Archer boys to the cleaners in the meantime! And talk of the Devil; here's our jockey now."

James Davies approached his boss and the owners of his sole ride of the day. He'd already had a surreptitious word with the waiter on the door of the box to ask how long was left until lunch was served. It wouldn't do to outstay his welcome.

Back in the Arkle bar, Dan and Mark had enjoyed three pints of Guinness each and a bottle of Champagne. The first race was only half an hour away. Dan was both tense and excited.

If there was ever a place to win money, it had to be Cheltenham or Royal Ascot, he thought. He'd had a large ante-post bet on the first race, the Supreme Novices Hurdle. Mark had had information from his father in Ireland, a passionate racing fan, that Kissane, the 4/1 favourite, had been working brilliantly at home and was very strongly fancied. Dan had called the Archer Brothers Racing Office in Walthamstow the week before and had £3,000 to win at 4/1, which included £50 for Mark.

Ante-post bets are wagers that are placed before the final declarations of any given big race are made. Betting ante-post can provide value for money, as the odds are likely to become shorter after the declarations are made, with some fancied horses likely to have been withdrawn.

Conversely, the risk of betting ante-post is that the punter loses his money if his selection is not entered at the final declaration stage. Dan had no worries on that score at least, as Kissane was not only a definite starter, he'd also been further backed into clear 3/1 favouritism.

They drained the remains of the Black Velvet and headed out of the packed Arkle bar towards the betting ring.

"Time for a little top up, mate," Dan said to Mark as they stood in front of the Archers' pitch. "Those idiots are laying Kissane at 7/2."

The Archers were indeed showing a standout price of 7/2 whilst most of their rivals were a slightly skinnier 3/1.

"Don't you think you've done enough already, Danny boy?" Mark suggested, turning to Dan. His words fell on deaf ears, however: Dan had vanished. Looking round the crowd at the Archers' pitch,

Mark soon spotted his colleague in discussion with Joss Archer, who took a drag of his cigar and shouted out "TWENTY-EIGHT HUNDRED TO EIGHT HUNDRED, KISSANE, DOWN TO BOY." Mark grimaced.

Dan reached for the diary in his right-hand pocket, the same diary that he kept a record of all his bets and a note of how much he was owed by, or more commonly that he owed to, the Archer Brothers. His latest investment of £800 stood to net him a profit of £2,800. This was on top of the £3,000 he'd placed last week, ante-post at 4/1.

Yes, this is going to be my day, he thought. £14,800; enough to shut that lairy bookmaker up.

The day was cold and sunny. Dan, surveying the blue sky above, was feeling contented. He was very excited and in a fine mood at what might lie ahead that afternoon. It was the typical optimism of a gambler, blissfully ignorant of lurking horror ahead.

Chapter Ten

Dan and Mark squeezed their way through the hoards of punters in the betting ring and into the members enclosure. From his vantage point on the lawn, Dan could see Kissane parading up the track to his right. A big rangy gelding, he had the physical attributes of a boxer. He looked imposing, almost arrogant.

Dan looked at his Racing Post to see who owned the beast and saw that Kissane was the property of a Miss Aisling O'Connell. He wondered if she was as nervous as he felt. He wondered if her heart was pumping as fast as his. He doubted it. She probably didn't owe two hard-nut East End bookmakers £7,500. The prospect of the debt rising to over £11,000 made him feel sick.

He remembered the last time he'd been in this kind of trouble, and how he'd recovered the situation by committing a criminal offence. There would be no more insider dealing now. Since his bollocking from Sir Marcus, he was a marked man. He needed winners – today.

He tried to brace himself for whatever outcome there might be. At school he'd read Rudyard Kipling's poem *If*. Dan remembered the famous words about triumph and disaster and treating 'those imposters just the same'. He wasn't sure that in his gambling he could treat the two imposters equally.

There were people amongst the scrum on the lawn that he recognised, but the last thing he felt like at 1.55pm that afternoon was socialising with any of them.

Mark guessed how Dan was feeling, and decided to keep his own counsel, at least until after the race.

"Hey, Dan, m'boy. I thought I'd see you here." Dan heard the voice of Sir Marcus Holderness directly behind him. He turned around to see a jovial looking Sir Marcus and Diana beaming at him. He inwardly grimaced, but outwardly he faked a smile while he shook Marcus's hand and kissed Diana on both cheeks. He prayed they'd go away.

"We're watching down there," said Marcus, vaguely pointing to a spot beyond. "Must rush as they're nearly off, but why don't you and your friend join us in Box 147, Neville Taylor's, after the race?" He glanced at Mark. "We can do the introductions later, but the captain told me that if I found any waifs and strays, I could ask them to come up after lunch."

After a moment's hesitation, Sir Marcuss leaned forwards and spoke in a low, conspiratorial voice to Dan. "Your dad won't thank me for saying this, but I may as well tell you that the good captain has advised me to have two decent bets on our horse, one for himself and the other for me."

Then Marcus straightened, smiled, and led his wife away. Whilst relieved they'd gone, Dan was pleased to have got the invitation to the box, and absolutely delighted about the Beacon Boy tip. He'd thought about backing the horse earlier, but now armed with that information he'd *have* to go in large.

He looked at Mark and managed a wry smile. "Can't ignore info like that, mate. It's from the horse's mouth!"

Mark raised his eyebrows and shook his head. "You must have a death wish," he said.

The starter called the jockeys to line up. The butterflies and apprehension that Dan had been briefly relieved of from the recent intervention of Sir Marcus and Diana, returned in force.

"They're off."

The tapes rose and a massive roar went up from the crowd, thousands of English and Irish punters full of hope and expectations. Triumph or disaster. Kissane got away well and was in fourth place as the twenty runners jumped the second flight of hurdles. Dan felt content. He was sure that the horse would stay the trip easily.

"Keep her up there," he murmured. He didn't want to see Kissane get boxed in behind the pack.

So far so good. The pace was strong and Kissane had a high cruising speed. They were over the fourth from home. The pressure was on. Running down the far side of the course, Dan's hopes were rising.The runners reached the top of the hill and swung left handed into a dip before getting to the straight and then the exhausting climb up the hill to the winning line. They were over the third last. Second now and challenging for the lead. Still travelling powerfully. The Irish start to roar their favourite home. They were into the home straight. Kissane took up the running.

"Come on Kissane! No danger!" screamed Dan. The noise

level would have surpassed that of any cup final. Kissane was joined in between the final two hurdles by three challengers.

"Fight back, you bastard."

"They're turning on the tap," roared the commentator. "Kissane being attacked on all sides. Tartan Tailor cruises to the lead. Kissane dropping away."

Tartan Tailor, a 14/1 chance, was the winner. Kissane did indeed drop away, rather badly beaten by sixteen lengths.

"Disaster," murmured Dan. He felt like he was going to crumble in disappointment. All the fun of the day dissipated instantly.

Mark tried to console him. "Mate, there's still Beacon Boy to come. As your man told us, it's straight from the horse's mouth, and in this case 'the horse's mouth' is one of the top trainers in the country. At least back it to win your stake back on Kissane."

After a few more minutes, Mark and Dan walked off in different directions, having agreed to meet back in box 147. Mark said he'd follow him up there after joining the long queue for the gents.

Over an hour later there was no sign of Mark. Dan felt embarrassed when asked by Sir Marcus who his friend was, and more importantly where he was?

Dan put this thought out of his mind as he mulled over his life. He should be having fun. It certainly looked like everyone else was. He thought about his life, his job. About Ciara. About his gambling. Was he out of control? He'd recently been taking his gambling more seriously than his career.

In the box he'd heard Captain Neville Taylor ask Sir Marcus to place a wager of £500 to win on Beacon Boy with the Archer Brothers. The captain had written his account number on a piece of paper and handed it to Sir Marcus, asking him to invite the brothers up for a brandy and a cigar whenever they pleased that afternoon when he placed the bet.

It wasn't lost on Dan that it was hardly ideal that his father's old friend was getting closer and closer to the Archers. He knew he wouldn't be able to pay if Beacon Boy failed to do the business. What would the Archers do then? They'd soon find out, probably that afternoon, that Sir Marcus Holderness and his dad were old friends. They'd no doubt mention any non-paid debts to Marcus before any 'alternative' action was to be taken. Gambling debts were not enforceable by law. Dan wondered what the alternative might be.

Probably a couple of broken kneecaps, he thought sadly.

When Sir Marcus had returned to the box, having duly placed the wagers, Dan made his excuses and left the room. He walked down the stairs and outside, then back up to the rails where Joss Archer was in full flight.

"SEVEN TO TWO BEACON BOY, SEVEN TO TWO I'LL LAY," the man shouted. Dan pushed his way through the crowd to the front of the queue.

"Hello son. What can I do for you?" said Archer, with just a hint of disapproval about him. Dan thought of the ever-burgeoning debt.

"Any chance of a bit of 4/1 on Beacon Boy?" asked Dan just as another punter thrust £600 in cash into Joss's hand, saying "£600 Beacon Boy at 7/2."

"SIX HUNDRED AT SEVEN TO TWO, BEACON BOY, TICKET EIGHT ONE TWO," shouted Joss back to his brother Wayne, handing the punter a ticket and adding "Three to one now, bruv."

Dan cursed. He remembered briefly backing a dog under not dissimilar circumstances at Walthamstow one night. Archer had helped him out there with the price. The result hadn't helped though.

"Joss, please mate, give me 7/2," he begged.

"How much?" came back the reply from the flamboyant bookmaker.

"£4,000 at seven to two."

Joss paused in his stride. "Are you sure, son? Your account is racking up a bit," he warned, but without waiting for Dan to reply shouted out to his brother, "FOURTEEN THOUSAND TO FOUR THOUSAND POUNDS BEACON BOY DOWN TO MR PERRY."

"Thanks Joss, appreciate it." said Dan.

"That's alright son, I know your good for it. You can pay me in the box later if by any chance it loses." Joss winked at him.

It was nearly four o'clock on the Tuesday of Cheltenham Races. The fourth race of the day was starting, a two-mile competitive handicap hurdle. It was overcast with a strong wind, a few specs of rain in the air.

Dan hadn't returned to the box. He couldn't bear the thought of confronting either of the Archers should the horse be defeated. He'd owe £15,300. What on earth would he do?

He stuck his hands in his coat pockets and walked out of sight of the bookmakers to find a suitable position to see the track. He needed to watch this race alone. He vaguely wondered where Mark had got to. He wasn't sure whether he was pleased or not that he'd disappeared.

Beacon Boy had looked good running down to the start; unflappable, on his toes, his chestnut quarters gleaming. He looked ripe and trained to the minute. Jamie Davies, the jockey, sported the blue and white hoops colours of Sir Marcus and Lady Diana. Dan felt his heart beating fast, trying to steel himself for what was to follow. Triumph or disaster. He couldn't deal with any more of the latter.

Down at the start, the runners circled each other warily. He wondered what instructions the captain had given Davies.

The starter called them in.

"They're lining up," called out the commentator. "And…they're off!"

Dan looked away from the runners initially, unable to stand the tension. He looked up from the proceedings towards the top of the hills in the distance.

Suddenly he didn't want to be there. He just wanted a happy life, away from this, maybe with Ciara. No more stress. No more gambling. Focus on his job instead. No more worrying about this stupid sport or the Archer Brothers or debts or the consequences of not paying them.

Scaramanga, a natural front runner, was the first to lead with Beacon Boy right there on his outside. James Davies had been told by Captain Taylor to ride his horse up with the pace and not to get left behind early. The ground was still officially good despite the drizzle of rain that had been falling for the last hour or so. Beacon Boy was not as experienced as some of his fourteen rivals, and Davies kept him up with the pace to give him a clear view of the hurdles and to reduce the risk of him falling in front of a stumbling competitor.

Dan was no longer watching. He knew that he'd leave straight away if the horse was beaten. He'd return to the town early and catch the early train back from Cheltenham to Paddington.

Fuck Mark, he thought. He listened to the commentary as he slowly edged his way towards the exit of the members' enclosure. Beacon Boy's jumping of hurdles was "smooth" he heard the commentator say. Still up there. Not much further. His hairs were standing up on the back of his neck.

"Please, God." Dan closed his eyes.

Beacon Boy made his first mistake at the second last when challenging for the lead. In horror, Dan turned to watch, but Davies had got the horse balanced again and was challenging strongly as the last flight approached. Scaramanga and Beacon Boy had pulverised their rivals and pulled ten lengths clear of the chasing pack. Captain Taylor's orders had been proven right. The crowd were in full cry.

Half a length down coming to the last Davies knew he had to go for a big one. He had the inside rail, the shortest but most perilous route, but victory was in sight.

And then it happened.

Scaramanga jumped the last in front, but Beacon Boy took off too soon and fell heavily, breaking his neck. He died instantly. James Davies got quickly to his feet and under the rail as the chasing pack thundered home, before hurling his whip to the ground.

Dan stood there wanting the ground to eat him up. At that point, he felt so miserable that he'd have almost chosen to give up his own life. He felt the panic begin like an engine revving up from his abdomen. Tension grew in his face and limbs, his mind replaying the horror of what he'd just witnessed. He became nauseas and short of breath.

In these moments after his personal hurricane, he understood his gambling addiction, but with hands trembling he still reopened *The Sporting Life* to look for any other last-chance saloon bets – anything to stop his primal urge, to get him out of this hell hole on the hills and to safety. The panic was still welling up within him as he desperately scanned the pages. He found a bench unattended on the lawn and lit a cigarette to try and calm himself.

Within seconds of trying to look for one last 'get out of jail' bet, he flung the newspaper onto the grass. Then the only movement his made was the trembling of his limbs and salty tears darkening his sleeves. He remained there, eyes closed, unaware of the passing afternoon.

"And the runners are going down to the start for our next race…" The commentator's words brought him back to himself, and he regained some composure. When he opened his eyes, it was to the descending remnants of the sun. He looked up at the sky, brilliant white against the blue.

He could still feel himself trembling, but he knew at that point he was not going to bet again that day, nor that week. Who knew how long until he placed his next wager? This could be the beginning of the rest of his life…or simply the end of it.

He took a very deep breath of the cold Cotswolds air, cursed out loud to the disapproving looks of a couple of elderly, tweeded-up lady racegoers, and stood up. He took another deep breath and started walking, briskly at first, off the lawn, out of the enclosure, then left onto the tarmac and up the hill, quickening his pace to a jog as he went. He wanted to be out of this racecourse and out of this game right now.

He left the exit behind him and took a cab from the rank up by the horseboxes opposite the racecourse. He told the driver to take him to Cheltenham Station, but once on their way he had a change of plan. Despite his leaving before the last race, he knew that he'd still have a long and boring wait at Cheltenham Station before the arrival of the next train. He could stop off at a pub for forty five minutes. He needed a drink.

He asked the driver to recommend a boozer.

The pub was huge and very crowded. There seemed to be so many televisions it reminded him of a trading floor, but with alcohol allowed. There were plenty of punters who'd left the track early, reading *The Sporting Life* and *The Racing Post*, hoping to back the winner of the next race. And there were the locals, mostly elderly, who used the betting shop in nearby Winchcombe Street. Same routine: pub – betting shop – pub – betting shop.

He ordered a large brandy and turned to look at one of the screens. An advert for *Yellow Pages*, then another one, this time the government promoting a public offering of shares in British Petroleum, available in October. Dan wondered where he'd be by then. He certainly wouldn't be in a position to buy any shares for a long while.

Before the racing resumed, a final advert caught his eye. There were images of a couple beaming with excitement at the news that they were being given a loan.

"GET A LOAN WITH THE HALIFAX, WITH THE HALIFAX," a pretty young thing in a suit was singing.

He ordered another brandy. He could sleep on the train. He lit a cigarette before noticing two men in deep conversation at a table the other side of the pub. A man, possibly in his sixties, with long dark hair and a wearing a suit was talking to a man with his back to Dan, at least thirty years his junior. They were getting rather animated, so much so that he could make out their Irish accents. The older man was shaking his head. The younger one picked up two empty pint glasses and headed to the bar to order more Guinness. As he did so Dan's jaw dropped.

The younger of the men was Mark O'Brien.

"You might have told me you were going to fuck off and leave me in the lurch," Dan said to his colleague.

"Mate, I'm so sorry," said Mark, turning a deep shade of red. "The trouble is after I left you in the Arkle, I bumped into my dad." He gestured in the direction of the long-haired man in a suit. "I'll get these. Come and meet him."

"I've heard so much about yer," said Kelvin O'Brien after Mark made the introductions.

Dan already thoroughly disliked the man now sitting in front of him. The expensive suit didn't go with the long black mane of hair, nor the brown boots, nor the tattoos that he sported on his neck.

"I had no idea he was coming over," Mark said to Dan, looking apologetic.

"Dat's roight," said his father in a broad Ulster accent. "I tort I'd come over since some of me pals were commin' over loike, and oi needed to com anyway what with som' business matters in London dat need attending to."

Dan asked what business he was in. Kelvin O'Brien stared at Dan directly in the face for a few seconds without answering. He didn't like Dan either.

Eventually he replied, "Oim a businessman, son. Leave it at that, oi say."

Another young man, about the same age as Mark, interrupted them. Another Irish accent. "Hi Mark," he greeted before addressing Mark's father. "I've got the car outside, Mr O'Brien."

"Oil be outside in a couple of minutes, Seamus," said Kelvin O'Brien as he got to his feet. He took two £10 notes from his pocket and gave them to Mark. "You boys have a few drinks on me on the way back. Oi'd offer you a lift, but the car's full, isn't that roight Seamus?"

"Yes, Mr O'Brien," replied his driver.

Kelvin O'Brien turned back to the boys and shook their hands, not looking Dan in the eye, before saying to Mark, "We'll talk in the week, right son?"

"So we will, Daddy," was the reply

The two men said little on the train returning to Paddington, partly as both had had a lot to drink and were content to sleep most of the way through the journey. Dan was furious with Mark anyway for both the ludicrous tip he'd passed on from that turd of a father of his, causing him to risk much more than he would have normally on the ill-fated

Beacon Boy, as well as going missing all afternoon and leaving him to make small talk with bloody Marcus and Diana. He downed the remainder of the brandy that he'd chosen from a man with a trolley, repleat with drinks, crisps, and sandwiches, and felt his heavy eyelids gradually unable to stay open. By the time the train had reached Swindon, both he and Mark were snoring.

At Paddington, after agreeing that they'd talk at work the following day, Dan hailed a cab. The cab arrived outside Ciara's flat at eight o'clock. He thought it would be best to ring on the buzzer to alert her that he was back rather than just letting himself in. He wanted so badly to talk to her about the day he'd had, the Archers, the O'Briens, the debt, and his plans to abandon betting. She'd help him give up. They'd do it together.

There was no reply. Dan cursed as he let himself in. Where was she? He watched the news. Surely she'd have told him if she was going out. She knew he'd be back that evening.

At ten he ordered himself a pizza. He watched a political documentary about the privatisation of national industries such as Cable and Wireless, British Telecom, British Petroleum, and British Gas.

Eleven O'clock. Still no sign of Ciara.

Shortly after midnight he heard a key in the latch. She was back. He wondered whether this was the right time to have a serious conversation with her, but opted to wait for another day. She was hardly in a chatty mood anyway.

When she explained rather impatiently that she'd been out to dinner with her father, who was over from Ireland, Dan's temper began to boil over. Out with her father, over from Ireland. Funny coincidence that.

She and Mark must think I'm fucking stupid, he thought. Mark's father over? Her father over? He remembered the times that he'd tried calling them at work, only to be told that neither were there. There was also the time when they'd disappeared all afternoon, that day he'd first taken Ciara down to the floor on the day of her interview. Mark had said that he'd introduced her to the other traders and let her go home before he sustained a migraine and went home himself. Dan hadn't believed him at the time. He hadn't directly asked Ciara about it since they'd started dating, as it appeared to hit a raw nerve in her every time Dan referred to the nature of her relationship with Mark.

And there was the night of the office party. Funny that the only two people in the department that hadn't made the event until after the explosion were Mark and Ciara.

She climbed into bed beside him. "Jesus, you stink," she said coldly, referring more to the stench of alcohol than Dan's hygiene.

Dan leaned to his side and switched on his bedside lamp. "I don't know what to think any more Ciara," he said. "Mark left me on my own after the first race and didn't come to the box that we were both invited to. I found him hours later in a pub in Cheltenham talking to an Irish guy who he claims is his father. Now you're coming up with the same type of bullshit.

.

"Now why don't you start telling me the fucking truth for once? You're shagging that Irish bastard too, aren't you? Well, fuck me, you've ballsed up your excuse this time. Where did Mark go to meet you after I left him at Paddington? You saw him didn't you?

"He introduces me to his arsehole of a father, shit they even look the same, then you come up with this fucking lie about going for dinner with your old man, who by an amazing coincidence is also over from Ireland. And you conveniently forget to tell me this until now because in reality you've been double dating that Irish wanker against me for ages. Oh, and just for good measure I've absolutely done my bollocks thanks to that Irish prick father's duff information."

Ciara's bottom lip was trembling. Dan had been prepared for her to try and hit him and intercepted her punch when it came, despite his inebriation.

"I hate you Dan. Fuck off out of my flat or I'll call the police, you bastard."

Dan needed no more asking. He pulled on his clothes and stumbled out of her flat and into the cold night air.

Chapter Eleven

April 1987

They ask you twenty questions.

Dan had undergone the questionnaire back in March, when he'd rung the Gamblers Anonymous 24-hour emergency helpline shortly after breaking up with Ciara. The lady had been understanding, comforting even. She'd listened to him as she'd listened to so many hundreds before. She was trained to let the caller spill out as much about his life as possible and how it was affected by gambling. After a while she asked him if he felt up to answering the questions.

"Do you or did you, lose time from work or when you were at school due to gambling?"

"Yes, both."

"Does gambling affect your reputation?"

"Yes. Everyone in the stock market and all my friends and family know I gamble."

"Do you ever gamble to get money with which to pay debts or otherwise solve financial difficulties?"

"Yes. I always try and gamble myself out of trouble."

"After losing, do you ever feel that you must return as soon as possible to win back your losses?"

"Yes, always."

"Have you ever committed an illegal act with which to finance your gambling?"

"Yes. Rather not say what though, if that's ok?" He wasn't going to risk telling a complete stranger about the Geneva Electric/Standard Telegram coup.

The questions continued. He answered 'no' a couple of times along the way, but the majority of answers were in the affirmative. He already knew that she was going to tell him that he was a head case, but it was the final question that silenced him.

"Have you ever considered self-destruction or suicide as a result of your gambling?"

Hot tears began welling in his eyes. He couldn't bring himself to answer the question. There was a pause.

"Hello, are you still there?"

Another pause. She'd expected it from this lad, suspecting that this case was worse than her usual callers. Those gamblers that were only borderline cases always automatically replied 'no' to question twenty.

"Y-yes, I'm still here," he eventually croaked. She didn't need to hear his answer to the final question. The final release. She already knew.

The evening following his conversation with the kind lady at

Gamblers Anonymous, Dan found himself walking down some steps of an old building near Westminster. It was quite clearly a school.

Probably a nursery school, he thought as he walked down the corridor looking for the assembly room. Children's paintings adorned the walls.

"Are you here for tonight's meeting?" asked a friendly face holding a clipboard. Dan replied that he was. "May I start by taking your name?"

Dan smiled for the first time in what seemed an age and replied, "Er, this is the Gamblers Anonymous meeting, isn't it?"

"Yes, my friend it is. Forgive me, I only meant your Christian name," the friendly face chuckled. "I'm Gerry. Tea and biscuits are over there, and the donations box is next to them. That's Lenny with the box. He's only there to make sure none of us are tempted to put the tea and biscuit money in the fruit machine at the pub later. You're welcome to join us for a drink after the meeting. After all, we're allowed to do that, eh, my friend.?"

Dan smiled. His mates would be at the Walthamstow dog races by now.

"Yes, I dare say we probably are, Gerry."

The meeting started. Gerry was standing at the podium with a microphone. He requested the audience to stand, and that they read aloud the serenity prayer used in Alcoholics and Gamblers

Anonymous meetings throughout the world.

"God, grant me the serenity to accept the things I cannot change, courage to change the things I can, and wisdom to know the difference. Amen."

The audience sat.

Gerry continued, "Welcome to all of you. We have most of our usual faces here tonight, but I'm delighted to say a couple of new ones too, so could you please give a welcoming hand to Maria and Dan." The audience clapped. Dan smiled. Maria blushed.

"Now I'm delighted to ask Robin to come forward and collect his two-year pin." Robin collected his award for abstaining from gambling for two whole years. More clapping.

"And this is a very special evening because I want you to give a really big round of applause to Gary who has earned his ten-year pin!" Thunderous clapping and cheers went up from the twenty or so strong contingent.

Dan wondered what it would be like never to gamble again. When he'd had those dark thoughts on the lawn during that disastrous day at Cheltenham, he'd vowed never to bet again, yet only a few days later he'd harbored strong desires to gamble. He'd related this to the lady on the Gambler's Anonymous helpline, who had assured him that this was very common. She'd recommended that he try going to a meeting, and to see if by sharing his experiences with others in a similar position, the temptation to return to gambling could be resisted.

"Great stuff, thank you," Gerry announced. "Now for the purposes of our new members, Maria and Dan, it's a tradition at these meetings that we offer new members the opportunity to say a few words about themselves first. You can be as long or short as you like.

"Don't forget, friends, that you have already made the first, brave step to your recovery merely by being here. I know that it can be intimidating talking to complete strangers about experiences that you've suffered in your gambling, but by sharing our experiences together we can find that inner strength to rebuild our lives.

"So, Maria, without any further a do would you care to come up to the podium and tell us a few words about your situation please, my luv?"

More applause. Everyone in the room turned to look at Maria, the only lady there. She was a middle eastern woman in her late thirties, expensively dressed and extremely beautiful. Dan recalled having recently read in the newspapers about an Arabian princess who had blown millions in the elite London casinos, Aspinalls, The Clermont Club, and Crockfords.

Was it her? he wondered. Suddenly an air of expectancy had fallen over the assembly as they waited for Maria.

"No, no, pleese, I so sorry. Not ready speek. Prefer to jus leesen," the woman stuttered.

Gerry quickly intervened. "Well, Maria, that's absolutely no problem whatsoever, my luv. I mean, my friend," he quickly corrected himself. "You can take things entirely in your own time. There's no obligation here."

He looked towards Dan. "Perhaps, Dan, you may like to say a few words?"

Now they all looked at Dan. He could see the question on their faces: *Would this one get up?* Dan got to his feet and walked up to the podium. Lots of clapping followed.

"Go on, Dan," beckoned a stranger's voice from the crowd.

"Well done, Dan," Gerry beamed, clapping him on the shoulder. "Now before you commence what you wish to share with us this evening, please could you both start and finish by telling us your name followed by, the words 'I am a compulsive gambler'."

Rather like the reading of the serenity prayer, Dan could not help feeling that this was a little silly. He wasn't even vaguely religious, and poor Maria had been made to recite the words of a Christian prayer when she was most likely a Muslim. Furthermore, Gerry had announced their names to the audience several times already. He saw Gerry as something of a cross between Arthur Daley and Bruce Forsyth, one a comical actor and the other a game show presenter of the time.

Still, he complied. "My name is Dan, and I am a compulsive gambler."

This was answered with lots of clapping. Dan looked at his audience. People from different backgrounds, different creeds. Different classes. All with one thing in common.

"It started when I was at boarding school. My parents had coughed up for me to go on a school trip to the opera in Covent Garden. A few of us saw this as an opportunity to abscond and spend a few hours drinking in London. One of my pals knew a seedy casino in Soho. I think it was illegal, as we had no trouble getting in and you need twenty-four-hours' notice to become a member at anywhere decent.

"Anyway, we blagged our way in, had a few drinks, and played roulette. I only had £25 on me, but despite buying some drinks I remember having over £150 by the time we got back on the coach.

"Needless to say, we got caught and sent to the Head. We were told that we'd only avoid expulsion if we were honest about where we'd been. We got sent home for a week during the term as punishment.

"During the following school holidays – it was Easter – my friends from the casino met up at the races. We were all with our parents as Easter Saturday at Plumpton Races is a big social occasion in Sussex. I remember each of the six favourites won, and I backed all of them.

"On the Bank holiday Monday I returned, this time on my own, and again returned home with my pockets bulging. I was truly bitten by now and spent the rest of my schooldays buried in *The Sporting Life*, which a day boy brought in for me each day. I spent every Tuesday, Thursday, and Saturday afternoon in a dingy betting shop whilst my peers would either be playing sport or revising for exams.

"At first some of us would venture off together to race meetings such as Brighton, Fontwell, or Goodwood, but the others didn't have the bug as bad as I had and eventually, I just went on my own.

"School finished. I failed all my A-Levels and didn't get a place at university or college. Not that I cared. All I wanted was a job which would pay me money that I could use for gambling.

"I got fired from my first job in the city due to gambling. It was Royal Ascot week and I'd pretended to be ill. Needless to say I was spotted at the racecourse by one of my bosses who was there legitimately.

"I got a new job as a junior in the stock market – a 'blue button'. I was good at it too, and quickly promoted. Trouble is, the more I got paid the more I gambled."

Dan told his audience about getting into debt, trying to gamble his way out of it, about the Archer brothers, the dogs. He felt comfortable here, in full swing, and even dared mention that he'd done 'something illegal' to fund his gambling. He spoke of his break-up with Ciara after the nightmare at Cheltenham and the depression and despair that followed.

He knew that he'd be back here next week and the week after. He was determined to sort his life out without gambling.

"My name is Dan. I'm a compulsive gambler," he finished.

Gerry, the leader of the meeting, watched Dan as he sat back down in his seat. The longer he'd attended these meetings, the better his perception had become as regards new members chances of 'remaining clean', though it never got any easier not to feel sorry for them, whoever they were, because it always reminded him of his own self destruction many years earlier. Made no difference if they were cleaners, rich Muslim women, or posh public schoolboys from the city; all had the same problem. He had an inclination that Dan might make it.

"Well done, Dan, you did yourself proud," said Gerry after the meeting was over.

Dan had to force himself not to break down in tears. Nobody had paid him a compliment in a while.

"Thanks Gerry. I'll see you next week," he replied.

Toxic Options

Chapter Twelve

Late April 1987 - December 1987

The final letter had come towards the end of April, preceded by two statements requesting that payment of £15,300 was to be remitted forthwith by cheque to Archer Bros. Ltd, Walthamstow. The letter had stated in a sinister tone that *THIS PAYMENT IS OVERDUE AND UNLESS YOUR REMITTANCE IS RECEIVED IN FULL, WITHIN 7 DAYS, FURTHER ACTION WILL BE TAKEN TO RECOVER FUNDS.* It was signed not by Joss or Wayne Archer but by an anonymous squiggle, underneath which it said *Accounts Manager.*

Dan had ignored the previous statements, subconsciously hoping that some miracle may suddenly befall him, but he knew that it was now time to confront the situation.

He'd been to the Gamblers Anonymous sessions each week since his first visit, sometimes twice if he'd been tempted to relapse, and had mentioned his debt to Gerry one evening over a drink. Gerry suggested that he tried to go and see the Archers in person, however scary it may seem.

To Dan's immense relief, Joss Archer could not have been more jovial on the phone when he'd made the call. Dan told him that he had couldn't afford to repay it all at once, but promised to make smaller, monthly payments until he had paid back the entirety of his debt. He asked Joss if they could meet for lunch one day to discuss terms as Walthamstow wasn't too far from the City.

Dan wasn't sure how serious Joss was being when he'd replied, "All right son, we'll work something out without me employing our 'traditional' methods of recovery, but I want to go to that City Circle place where all them birds wear stockings and suspenders…and you're going to foot the bill, skint or not."

The City Circle was a thriving restaurant near The Bank of England, where the most scantily dressed young waitresses served city gents long and boozy afternoon lunches.

To take Joss Archer there is going to be expensive, thought Dan, but he quickly understood that if they could come to an amicable agreement, it would be infinitely preferable to waking up on a Saturday morning at home to see his car burnt out, or to be confronted by heavies at any given time, employed to use the 'traditional' methods of debt collection.

Dan booked for 12.45 and arrived at 12.30. He did not think it would be smart to risk leaving Joss Archer waiting. The restaurant was already full of male bankers and stockbrokers in exuberant spirits that Friday afternoon. The only women present were the waitresses, who were exuding an air of sexuality about them as they hovered around tables like bunny girls in a strip joint.

He ordered a beer and looked about him, noticing that without exclusion all his fellow lunchers were dressed just like him – in sober suits and ties. He silently prayed that Joss would be similarly dressed so as not to show him up, but somehow considered that unlikely. Brash, loud, gaudy, Joss Archer.

How could I have got myself into this situation? he thought. It had been barely over a month since Cheltenham. He'd coped up until then, but now he was flat broke. At least he hadn't had a bet since. He wondered if he'd hit the 'rock bottom' that he'd heard his fellow sufferers refer to at Gamblers Anonymous.

He tried to predict how Joss would be here, outside his comfort zone. This place could hardly be any different to any racecourse restaurant let alone the bar at Walthamstow dog races.

As all these thoughts flew through his mind, he suddenly heard the noise level in the restaurant descend into an eerie silence. There were large marble steps that led from the entrance and reception of the City Circle at street level down to the restaurant below. Standing halfway down the marble steps was a man in his mid-forties sporting long blonde hair, an open necked shirt, and a large gold medallion. He was wearing a white suit and shirt and grey cowboy boots. He puffed on a large cigar as he surveyed the looks of the astonished lunchers beneath him before he spotted Dan, whereupon he broke into a broad grin.

"'ALLO, SON," he boomed. A ripple of nervous laughter emanated from the throng as Joss Archer joined Dan at the table, and it was quiet for a long few moments before the noise level returned to its previous volume.

The lunch went rather better than Dan had anticipated. Joss was clearly in his element and enjoying himself. Most importantly, he was conciliatory, and they came to an agreement that Dan's account with Archer Brothers would be closed, and that Dan should pay of a minimum of £500 per month until the debt was repaid.

Dan was overcome with relief. No need to take out another loan – he had enough of those already – and he'd quite comfortably be able to make the monthly repayments. He promised Joss that any bonus he received before the termination of the debt would be paid straight to Archer Brothers. He was very confident that the debt could be repaid by the end of the year, as he was contemplating taking on a trading position in the stock market that would make Sinclair Bank an absolute fortune, and ultimately net him a huge bonus. And this time it would be entirely legitimate.

The summer rolled on by. Dan remained committed both to his £500 monthly repayments and to attending regular meetings of Gamblers Anonymous. He threw himself into his work, always the first to get in each morning and the last to leave at night. His team were making big money as the stock market continuously hit new highs. His reputation in the bank soared as prices surged higher.

The bull market had started in the summer of 1982 and was still going strong, fuelled by lower interest rates, hostile takeover bids, leveraged buyouts, and a raft of corporate mergers, leading to companies raising huge amounts of capital to finance such deals. A leveraged buyout involved a company raising capital by selling bonds to the public. They paid high interest rates, as they were not guaranteed by the government and therefore carried a reasonable degree of risk. These were known as 'Junk Bonds'. IPOs were another feature of this bull market, with companies offering shares to the public for the first time at a discounted price.

This was also the very beginning of what was to become the technology boom. Investors had caught on to the idea that computers and technology would spur a feast of new business opportunities.

By the end of September that year, Dan noticed that both the analysts at Sinclair Bank, for whom he had little time, and the bank's equity traders had become almost blasé in their attitude to the direction of the stock market, talking as if it would never fall again. It was usually the case that even in a bull market, prices would correct themselves when traders, analysts, the media, and the general public were all of the same opinion. He knew that it wouldn't take much bad news to cause such a 'correction'.

With this in mind, Dan called a meeting of the bank's risk committee. He pointed out at the meeting that all the bank's equity books were heavily long of stock. Even his own option traders had very few short positions, although they had bought plenty of puts, downward 'bets', back in June when there had been a general election. A Labour win back then could have fuelled a major downturn, but the Conservatives prevailed, and the prices of those puts had largely evaporated.

Dan had an overpowering feeling that a wind of change was forthcoming. He told the risk committee that he wanted permission for his team to build substantial bear positions, at the very least enough to protect the bank in the event of a market downturn. He'd heard an old saying, 'When the dentists are buying, it's time to get out'; most of the great crashes in history occurred when the investing public were caught in the same bubble. This time it wasn't just the public but market professionals too, all of the same opinion. Bubbles burst. Markets crash.

The risk committee had taken a very short time to approve Dan's strategy. The two weeks leading up to Monday 19th October 1987 had been not particularly profitable for Sinclair Bank in general, but, due to Dan's strategy, at least the traded options department had outperformed, and severely limited losses sustained by other trading departments within the bank.

Sentiment in the markets seemed to have changed, although most investors considered that the turn around in prices was merely a short-term correction. Not Dan.

Ray Plewcinski, the head of the risk committee, was an American who had recently transferred to London from the New York branch of Sinclair Bank. He called Dan at home on the morning of 18th October.

"Hey buddy, sorry to call you on a Sunday morning, but have you seen what the Dow did on Friday night?" he asked, already having guessed that Dan would most certainly have known. A sharp fall on Wall Street had led to frenzied commentary in the weekend newspapers that something more sinister lay ahead.

"The treasury has threatened to de-value the dollar in order to narrow the US's ever expanding trade deficit. Looks like we may be in for a bloodbath tomorrow, Dan. You guys still short?"

"There was a full-on hurricane over here last Thursday night,

Ray," said Dan referring to the huge storm that had hit the UK three nights earlier. "All the electrics went down and the market over here was closed as a consequence all Friday, unable to react to the weak performance on Wall Street. That's going to cause extra panic. I think the strong current is going to precede a financial tsunami."

Dan went on to explain that his team were perfectly poised for any potential collapse in prices. Indeed, they were, as he'd instructed all of his traders to build large long put positions (down bets) straight after he'd got the risk committee's approval. Every stock that they covered in the traded options market, from oils and electricals, to retailers, miners and all industrials, Sinclair Bank's Option dealers were short, and with their burgeoning put positions created over the course of the last three weeks poised to explode in the case of a further, sharper, downturn.

Dan rose before 5am the following morning. He'd hardly slept due to the adrenaline coursing through him. The market hurricane, as opposed to the recent storms, was now due. Even before the UK Market had opened for trading that Monday morning, stock markets in and around Asia plunged. Investors moved to liquidate positions, creating a cascade of panic. The most severe case was New Zealand, which was down a horrifying 60%. A veritable tempest of a crash was now underway.

He was at his desk by 6am. For once he wasn't the first in, as most of the equity traders and analysts were aware of the weekend's events and had felt the need to be completely on top of their positions that Monday morning. The mood was tense amongst the equity traders, all of whom were heavily loaded up with stock, already battered over the previous few trading days and sure to get decimated when the market officially opened at 9.00 am.

After an earlier than usual morning meeting with heads of each relevant desk, Dan decided to walk down to the floor for the opening, as he felt he'd be better employed keeping watch over his own traders there. He also wanted to watch history in the making.

Dan had never seen anything like it before. The atmosphere was electric – not like Cheltenham, this was different. Traders and brokers with real fear etched on their faces.

The bell rang and all hell let loose. Back up in the offices, not just at Sinclair but at all the other banks, many traders were refusing to take incoming calls so as to avert taking on more stock from panicked shareholders. Nobody knew the right price of anything. The normally orderly market had been thrown into total confusion – it was chaos, with wild fluctuations in prices.

The panic ensued in the traded options market. Dan moved from sector to sector, telling his traders to keep calm amongst the furore and not to deal in large size. He was aware that his team were making a fortune and that it would be easy to buy all the positions back quickly as an ocean of sell orders hit the market, but this was history in the making and panic and fear were the order of the day.

They would buy stock back at heavily discounted levels, only buying in decent size when orders to sell considerably below the market price came in. There were periods during the course of the day when share prices rallied as investors considered the market over-sold, but these rallies were short lived, and prices soon dipped lower again as waves of red covered the trading screens.

By the close of play that day, over £300 billion had been wiped off the value of the FTSE 100 constituents, rendering the FTSE over 300 points lower – a 24.4% loss that exceeded, in percentage terms, even that of the great crash of 1929.

The closing bell at 3.30 marked the close of the options session that day. The floor resembled the aftermath of a great battle; some wounded, some dead, some triumphant. All moved by the experience. It had indeed been history in the making.

Dan knew that his own personal financial problems were likely to be over. He could hardly wait to see how much his lads had made on his strategy. A lot of the positions, the majority of them in fact, had been unwound throughout the course of that manic day, leaving the department's exposure to whatever the market held in store over the next few days relatively small. When the profits and losses were totted up collectively, the options team, including Dan's own positions, which he took on a proprietary basis, amounted to just short of £1,200,000. The equity traders had lost just short of a million.

Dan's strategy had effectively saved the day. The press described that memorable day as 'Black Monday'.

Two weeks later, Dan was called into a meeting by Ray Plewcinski. "Hey, buddy, how do you fancy becoming a director of this place?" he said. "And don't make it difficult for me. From the size of the bonus that you're due, it would be kinda rude to pay so much money to someone who's not a director."

Dan was paid a bonus of £100,000 on December 1st. Having banked the cheque he called Joss Archer and invited him to lunch again at the City Circle. He explained that he had good news.

Joss appeared more formerly attired the second time. Dan grinned as he handed him an envelope with a cheque inside, exactly covering the remaining balance of his debt. Joss took a swig from his gin and tonic and dragged on his cigar before opening the envelope.

"I figured it might be this," said Joss, clearly impressed. "Just didn't expect it so soon. Told you I always get my money in the end, eh?"

Dan smiled, somewhat nervously.

Joss continued, "Now that you're back in the land of the living, son, I'm not going to recommend that you reopen your account, although I won't stop you if that's what you really want. I think you should stay away from gambling for a while."

"I'm not coming back, Joss," said Dan earnestly.

"Pleased to hear it, son. Now listen up. Wayne and I are giving a dinner, a Christmas dinner, if you like, for all our best clients, later in the month." He paused. "Alright, it's not exactly 'our' party, but the tickets were well difficult to come by. I got them off another punter in my debt – a member of the Jockey Club, no doubt terrified that a scandal would break if it got out that he had acquired huge gambling debts. And this buys my silence until he's come to an arrangement like you did.

"It's going to be well posh – black tie and held in The Grosvenor House Hotel in Mayfair. The whole of racing's glitterati will be there, including that Captain Taylor. Your mate Sir Marcus and his wife have accepted. I'd like you to come as a mark of how grateful I am to you for coughing up this fast. Wayne and I would love to see you there."

"Wow, sounds great," said Dan.

"And you need to bring a bird," Joss added.

Dan thought before replying. "I have someone in mind already. Someone at work that I used to go out with, but I'm not sure if she's in a relationship or not at the moment." His mind momentarily flashed to Mark O'Brien.

The niceties over, they got down to the serious business of studying the waitresses and devouring more bottles of wine than Dan cared to remember on waking up the following day. Joss asked about Dan's life and his work – and his sex life. Dan replied that he hadn't had much on that front since he parted with Ciara, but pointed out that he still saw her each day in a work capacity. Joss suggested that he brought her to the party at the Grosvenor and Dan replied that he'd thought just the same. They talked for hours; Dan was fascinated to hear about Joss's life, and more about the bookmaking business.

Joss was telling Dan about the robbery at the White City all those years ago when suddenly, something that Joss said made Dan sit upright.

"What did you say they were wearing when they attacked you? Did you say Mrs Thatcher masks? The two people the police are looking for from last years' attack on our party at Tower Bridge were spotted wearing the same, whilst they were running from the scene."

"She's a popular lady with some, that Mrs Thatcher," said Joss.

Dan felt uneasy about the coincidence. Not every violent crime was committed by offenders wearing Mrs Thatcher masks. However, at Joss's words he passed off the thought.

Chapter Thirteen

December 1987

Dan was a reformed man. He reflected how different his life was since he'd quit the gambling. Here he was, affluent, the youngest ever director of Sinclair Bank and with a spectacular career in front of him.

Part of him still missed the betting – particularly going to Walthamstow or the racecourse, but whenever he had serious pangs he'd return to Gamblers Anonymous as soon as possible, in addition to his regular weekly visit.

He felt regret over the insider dealing incident that he'd been persuaded to partake in by Mark O'Brien. Over a year had gone by since that dark episode in his life. He'd read in *The Financial Times* that an investigation had taken place, but the Securities And Futures Association had found no hard evidence of insider dealing and had closed the case. He had been desperate at the time, and luckily nothing came of it. How grateful he was that Sir Marcus had intervened, otherwise it may have become a habit.

His relationship with Mark O'Brien had cooled. They no longer drank together, but instead they maintained a strictly professional relationship and Mark's own performance as an options trader had been highly satisfactory.

Part of Dan had wanted Mark to underperform. He'd never forgiven him for shagging Ciara, as he believed, and still felt betrayed by the lies that they'd concocted behind his back. How convenient it would have been to have been able to 'let him go', as was the expression used to mean that someone was fired. He really didn't like Mark one bit and most definitely didn't trust him. He wasn't in the least surprised that his father was so revolting, a hard, unpleasant, Irish thug that in no way could have been Ciara's dad. He wasn't even totally sure that he was Mark's father, although they did admittedly look similar. He couldn't understand why Ciara had so obviously lied to him about having dinner with her own father that dreadful night after Cheltenham, unless of course, as he suspected, she'd actually been with Mark instead.

He'd asked other people on the floor surreptitiously if Mark and Ciara were an item, but no one seemed to know for sure. If they were, they were obviously covering it up.

The one thing missing from Dan's life was a girlfriend and at that particular point in his life, he knew that the only girlfriend he wanted was Ciara.

Ciara had also performed well and was no longer a blue button. Dan had been quick to promote her shortly after their break up, possibly too quickly, for the promotion hadn't been entirely due to the progress that she'd made as a trader. Not only did Dan think she'd be grateful to him for this hike in seniority, it also gave him the opportunity to move her to a different sector, as far away as possible from the electricals crowd and Mark O'Brien. Perhaps, now that she ran her own book in the stores sector, right across the floor from the electricals, it would ensure she spent less time in Mark's company.

As confident as Dan was at trading the markets, he was

anything but confident of winning Ciara back. He was also more than a little shy of asking her to the Archers' bash at the Grosvenor House Hotel. What if she said no?

One weekend he visited his parents in the country, and over a Sunday lunch pint in the local pub he told his father about his dilemma. Brian Perry listened intently to his son's predicament and had no doubt regarding his advice.

"Have some bollocks m'lad," he told his son. "You won't lose anything if she says no, and if she does you'll know where you stand. If she makes an excuse then at least she'll know that you're interested and then the prerogative is on her to give you the right signals. Either way, you'll go mad wondering what might have happened if you don't ask.

"You ask your mother. We went through the same rigmarole when we were courting. Best thing I ever did asking her out to tea. And I mean tea, not dinner. It was during the blitz. I asked her in The Strand tube station one night when the Luftwaffe were giving us another pounding. You've got it easy sunshine!"

Armed with his father's advice, Dan's mind was made up. He called Ciara that Sunday night and was relieved, if not a little nervous, when she picked up the phone.

"Hey Ciara, how's it going?"

"Dan?"

"How do you know it's me?" Dan replied somewhat tamely.

"I'd recognise that star trader's accent anywhere. Am I in trouble or something?"

"Er, actually I wanted to give you an invitation. To a party."

They were on the phone for the best part of an hour, catching up on each other's lives outside work since the day she'd sent him packing from her flat. They spoke freely and with good humour.

Ciara had already heard on the grapevine that Dan had stopped gambling. He'd even jovially made a reference to his Gamblers Anonymous meetings one day, whilst studying her trading positions in the stores sector. He explained about the recent lunch at The City Circle with Joss Archer and the reasons he'd been invited, but carefully refrained from asking her if she was in a relationship, let alone make any reference to Mark O'Brien.

"So, will you come? As my guest?" asked Dan, eager to ensure that she was in no doubt as to his intentions. He definitely noticed a moment's hesitation, a tad too long for his liking, before she accepted.

The 1987 Jockey Club dinner was planned for the Friday before Christmas at the magnificent Grosvenor House Hotel, Mayfair.

On Thursday morning, the day before the dinner, the stock market was already in Christmas holiday mode and trade was light in the extreme, with plenty of city employees having been out the previous night. Dan sat with his feet up on the desk reading a copy of *Mayfair*, a semi-porno glossy magazine, whilst occasionally peering at his screens.

He finished his coffee, chucked *Mayfair* aside, and put his shoes and suit jacket on before walking down to the Stock Exchange.

The London Options Clearing House was an office in Throgmorton Street manned by a clerical team of about ten staff. They provided detailed computer print outs showing the positions every bank or trading house had in each option on a daily basis. It was the onerous task of a blue button to make sure he was at LOCH by 7am each day in order to hand deliver these print outs both to the Sinclair Bank dealers on the floor and then to Dan back up in the head office in Broadgate. Each time that Dan visited the floor he would have already spent some time examining his traders' positions by way of these print outs, and made notes indicating where, in his opinion, a position was too big, too small, or needed to be closed down.

That Thursday morning, he followed his usual routine and, armed with the documentation, he spent a few minutes chatting with each of the traders. He'd decided to leave the Stores positions until last so that he could have a chat with Ciara and discuss where to meet the following night, but on walking across to her pitch he was slightly surprised not to see her there trading, or at least studying her positions.

A trader from another Bank said to him, "If you're looking for Ciara, mate, don't bother. She's gone home sick."

"Nice of her to tell me," Dan replied, his heart sinking. "Thanks for letting me know."

He'd look pretty foolish if he turned up to the Grosvenor House the following night alone, and Joss would be sure to poke fun at him. Optimistically, he considered it better to be today that she chose to be ill rather than tomorrow. He wondered if she just had a hangover.

He decided to call her and made the short walk out of the exchange and across the road to the Sinclair Bank 'box', a room where the Option traders resided outside trading hours during the day. He placed his LOCH print outs on a desk and dialled her number.

"You have reached Ciara Rogers. I'm not here at the moment, but please leave your message and time of your call after the tone. Thank you."

Irritated, Dan clicked off the phone and returned to the office. He'd try again later.

By 6pm he'd called her a further ten times, all to no avail.

Ciara certainly has her moments, but is just not unprofessional, he thought, getting increasingly frustrated. His frustration only intensified when he suddenly realised that he'd left his LOCH print outs and notes back in the trader's box . He swore. Now he'd have to go all the way back to the box to pick them up.

He knew that the traders would all be either in the pub or on their way home by this stage, so decided to return to Throgmorton Avenue and retrieve the print outs now rather than later. He hoped that one of the traders would have noticed that he'd left them and locked them away for safe keeping, but it was not a chance he could take. He would not risk leaving them unattended.

As he'd expected, there was nobody in the box when he arrived there at 6.30pm. There was no sign of the print outs either. He decided to check the trader's drawers, feeling slightly guilty about doing so. He resolved to turn a blind eye to anything inappropriate he might find.

Nothing in Kevin's drawer, nothing in Dave's. He opened Clive's drawer to find nothing but dirty socks, boxer shorts, and a dirty shirt. He winced at the smell. Dirty stop out. He continued his search. Nothing, nothing, nothing.

When he got to Mark O'Brien's desk, he noted that it was the only drawer so far to be locked. They must surely be in there, he thought. He'd just have to leave it until morning and come back for them then. He sat down in Mark's chair and turned on a screen to check the latest movements on Wall Street. He started jabbing at a keyboard that turned the pages of the screen, taking in various share prices that had a bearing on Sinclair's own positions. One of them was going slightly against them. He hit his fist on the desk in frustration, partly due to the price but also in annoyance that he couldn't find his notes, written on the missing LOCH sheets.

Also, Ciara.

As he leaned over to turn off the screen, he noticed that when hitting the desk, he'd slightly knocked the keyboard askew. This had dislodged a small key: the key to Mark's drawer. Relieved, Dan took the key and unlocked the drawer.

When he pulled it open, he gasped at what lay before him. Inside was an unopened white shirt, still in its packet, and a black bow tie. A pair of polished black lace up shoes lay next to them, but there was more.

Behind the shoes at the back of the drawer, Dan found himself looking at four sinister looking revolvers. He instantly recognised their makes, remembering from his history lessons at Lancing the choice of arms used by the IRA in the 1970s. Two were C96 Mausers, the others Colt 45 automatics.

Trembling, he opened the smaller drawer, where traders usually kept pencils and stationery. The pencils and stationery were neatly laid out at the top of the compartment. Underneath these, the drawer was lined with live bullets.

He lit a cigarette and rapidly considered his options. He had to talk to Ciara. Or should he go straight to the police station in Bishopsgate? He certainly didn't want to hang around here. What if Mark came back?

He quickly shut the drawers, relocked them, and replaced the key back underneath the keyboard. Ciara's desk was by the door of the box, the only one he hadn't opened. It was unlocked. He decided to take a peek. Nothing in the top compartment except lipstick, pencils, mints, and other assorted stationery. He swung open the bottom compartment. What he saw left him shaking with concern.

If he'd been shocked to discover the pistols and ammunition in Mark's drawer, to see what lay in Ciara's disturbed him just as deeply. No guns, no bullets – just a bunch of ten masks. All bearing the face of Mrs Margaret Thatcher, grinning upwards at him, lying on his LOCH computer print outs.

There was a bank of public payphones around the corner from The Stock Exchange. Dan ran the short distance and dialled Ciara, only to reach her answer machine yet again. He breathlessly left a message.

"Ciara it's me. We must talk. Please call me urgently at home." He deliberately didn't say what was so urgent, as he wasn't sure about the relevance of the masks. He wanted to see her reaction when he asked her why she had them.

He felt distinctly uneasy. He recalled Joss Archer describing the time he and his brother were attacked by Irishmen in Mrs Thatcher masks. And then there was the police report after the Tower Hill bombing that indicated witnesses seeing two men in the same masks, running from the scene of the crime.

Now certain that Mark O'Brien was up to no good, Dan wanted to find out for sure what was going on. He changed his mind about going home and awaiting her call – better to go straight to her flat and catch her off guard. These thoughts preoccupied his mind as he hurried to catch a taxi. He dreaded the thought of getting to her flat and finding O'Brien there but decided that he could always run – he'd go directly to the police in that scenario.

At least he knew that Mark's guns were secure in his desk. He also knew that neither Ciara nor Mark would have any idea what he'd found in the box earlier and would therefore be unaware of his suspicions.

Ciara's flat was in Fulham. The black cab slowly trundled through the London evening traffic. Blackfriars, Embankment, Westminster, Victoria, Sloane Square. Then onto the Fulham Road and past his own flat, then Stamford Bridge, Fulham Broadway.

They were very close. Dan was scared. He hadn't felt like this since Cheltenham, back in March.

The cab entered Ciara's road and he asked the driver to stop thirty yards from her flat, which was on the ground floor of a Victorian mansion block. He noticed that lights were on.

This is it, he thought as he firmly pressed the buzzer. No reply. He tried again to no avail. Unsure what to do next, he was pleased to find the front door of the mansion block opened by an elderly lady leaving the premises.

"Excuse me," said Dan. "Do you live here?"

The old lady smiled at him. "Yes, young man, who are you looking for?"

Dan told her.

"Yes, I saw Ciara only this morning. Such a lovely young girl. She sometimes comes and has coffee with me on Sunday mornings."

Dan explained that he was a friend of hers from work and

was concerned that she'd gone home earlier without any explanation and hadn't answered any of his calls.

"Well, let's have a peek from the outside," said the old lady. She led Dan round to near the front window, which was open a few inches. No sign of Ciara, but they could distinctly hear music emanating from the flat.

"Perhaps we should try knocking on her front door?" the old lady suggested, clearly only too pleased to help. They went back inside the building and Dan banged heavily on the door, the music louder from inside. If there was anyone there, they weren't in answering mode.

She is probably in her bedroom shagging that horrible Mark, Dan thought gloomily.

The old lady said, "I think we should speak to the caretaker. He lives in the basement. I know he's in as I just spoke to him a few minutes ago about people putting their rubbish bags out too early. Such a nuisance. Attracts rats you know, dear."

Ten minutes later Dan and the old lady were back inside the building, this time with the caretaker, who had keys to all the flats on his watch.

"I hope you're not makin' a big mistake, Mister," said the caretaker in a broad West Country accent. "Folks get right pissed off if I enter their premises when it's not an emergency."

"You won't need to. I shall go in alone," replied Dan.

"I ain't lettin' you in alone mate, you might be one of them burglars. Then I'd be in the shit. I'll come in too, if you don't mind."

The old lady winced at the bad language, but smiled at Dan. "I'm going to be late for my bridge night, so must be off. I hope Ciara's ok," she said as she turned away from the two men and headed back towards the main front door of the block.

The caretaker let himself into the flat, followed by Dan. The music really was quite loud. A pair of Ciara's shoes were lying loose by one of the sofas in her living room, and a skirt lay on the floor.

Dan called out to her. Nothing. He looked in the kitchen, where there were definitely some signs of recent activity. He saw a half-eaten sandwich in its wrapper and an open bottle of vodka, half empty.

He was dreading going into her bedroom, but walked down the passageway towards it, closely followed by the caretaker.

"Here goes," he said. Dan took a deep breath then knocked on the door. "Are you in there Ciara? I've been so worried about you. Are you ok?"

No answer.

"She ain't here mate. Best we leave, pronto," said the caretaker. After a minute. Ignoring him, Dan turned the door handle and gingerly peered into the room.

He took a few seconds to take in the scene. Ciara was in bed engulfed by hundreds of sleeping pills. By the side of the bed lay a

C96 Mauser and a Colt 45 automatic.

In a state of total shock, Dan stared uselessly at the corpse. The caretaker realised what had happened immediately. He told Dan to stand aside as he felt Ciara's pulse.

"She's still alive. Go on son, call a fuckin' ambulance."

Toxic Options

Chapter Fourteen

The medical term used by doctors to describe a stomach pumping is 'gastric lavage'.

The ambulance arrived within minutes from the nearby Charing Cross Hospital. The paramedic rushed to Ciara's side and examined her eyes, pulse, and breathing whilst an ambulance technician scooped the loose pills from the bed and placed them in a plastic bag.

Satisfied that not only was she alive, but that the overdose had happened relatively recently, the paramedic knew that it was likely Ciara could be saved. Gastric lavage rarely fails to work if a patient is treated within four hours of taking an overdose.

Ciara was lucky. Had she spent the night like that, she'd either have died or suffered chronic liver failure. The paramedic and ambulance technician delicately rolled Ciara onto one side and gently slid her from the bed onto a stretcher.

The paramedic asked if she could hear him. "Try and open your eyes, Ciara. What made a lovely girl like you do this to yourself?"

When she remained unresponsive, he turned to Dan and asked if he knew of any reason that Ciara should try and take her own life. Dan didn't know. He'd certainly never known Ciara to be severely depressed. All he knew was that she was caught up in something she shouldn't be, and this was the end result. However, he wasn't going to explain any of this to the paramedic, certainly not before he'd told to police. He wanted to get the truth from Ciara by himself.

She wouldn't be accompanying him to the Grosvenor House tomorrow, that was for sure.

In the ambulance she opened her eyes and emitted a long groan. Dan reached for her hand, which she gripped fiercely before bursting into choking, almost hysterical tears. The ambulance technician took out a small syringe and pricked Ciara's arm to sedate her whilst the other staff in the ambulance all used soothing words of comfort and reassurance.

"Ok Ciara, we're nearly there now."

"Don't worry love, you're in safe hands."

"Things will get better for you love."

They all knew that weeks of counselling and therapy lay ahead for Ciara. Would it work though? So many failed suicide attempts resulted in the patient repeating the process.

At the Charing Cross Hospital, the paramedic explained to Dan the process involved in gastric lavage surgery and told him that he'd be better off going home that night as Ciara would be better talking to him the following day.

Dan did not manage to get any sleep that night. He needed Ciara to talk to him, to tell him the truth. How much clearer would the situation be then?

He didn't have to wait long. He was back at the hospital at 8am the following day and used a telephone box to call in at the office to explain that he would be late. He didn't mention Ciara.

Then Dan checked with reception to see which ward Ciara was in and was told to take the lift up to Floor 3 and ask for the Ward Sister.

"She's fine physically, at least she will be sooner rather than later. She's very distressed however. She's been asking for you", said the Ward Sister.

Suicide patients were allowed a single room next to the ward for some privacy while they recover, at least for a day or so after admission. It was hardly luxury however. No telephone, no television, nothing with wires. There were bars on the window and there was a cupboard without hangers. A nurse would look in every hour.

The Ward Sister led Dan into the private room Ciara was in.

"Hi Ciara, sweetie. Someone's here to see you," she said in the gentle, cheerful tone one uses with the mentally fragile. She turned to Dan. "I'll leave you both alone for now."

The Ward Sister left, leaving Dan and Ciara staring at each other in silence. Ciara's eyes were red from crying. It wasn't long before Dan broke the silence. "Thank God I found you in time last night."

He sat on the chair beside her bed. Ciara started crying again.

Then between sobs she spoke.

"Hold me, Dan."

He was as gentle as possible as he held her close. She continued to sob.

"Dan. I'm so sorry. I've done something awful. So awful that I've put both of our lives in terrible danger."

He sat back, taking her hand in his so he didn't have to release her completely. "Your life's not in danger, my love," he reassured her. "The Sister told me herself."

There was a brief pause before he ventured, "The reason I came to your flat last night was that I knew something very sinister was happening.

"Ciara, listen baby, I know how much you hate me saying this, but if you're involved in anything, anything at all, with Mark O'Brien it's vital you tell me the truth. You're alive, I'm alive, and we'll stay alive if you explain to me what's going on."

Ciara had stopped crying now and wiped the tears from her face. "Ok Dan, I'm going to tell you everything."

"Take as long as you need baby," said Dan, still holding her hand. He knew the truth was about to be revealed.

"Oh my God, I don't know how I got in so deep. I told you on that first day, when you took me down to the Stock Exchange after my interview, that I knew Mark from my days in Ireland as a kid. Well, that was true, and we did have fun with each other partying, drinking, enjoying the craic, but you see Dan, there was never anything more to it than that." She paused for a couple of seconds before revealing, "You see, Mark O'Brien is my older brother."

Dan was open mouthed. He certainly hadn't seen that coming. He even felt a pang of relief as he asked about her father.

"My daddy is a bad man. A very bad man. And you've met him. That night you came round to my flat after you'd lost your money at Cheltenham, I told you I'd been out to dinner with Daddy. I was going to tell you then, but you were so drunk that I wasn't going to explain all the facts to you that night, and then we had that fight, and then you left and we split up and-"

She started crying again. Dan got back on the bed and hugged her close.

"Just keep going, babe. Kelvin O'Brien is your father right?" Dan said slowly.

"He is that. You met him with Mark at Cheltenham, and I met up with the two of them when they'd returned back to London. He's a senior commander in the IRA. He was very strict with us as children. We attended mass every Sunday. We were taught to hate the British. Our Uncle was killed by British troops on Bloody Sunday in 1972.

"Anyway, it was expected of Mark and I to follow in Daddy's steps. We both came over to London in 1982 to join a newly formed IRA cell in London. We staged a robbery to raise money – on a couple of East End Bookies. The same bookies that invited you to the Grosvenor House Hotel tonight."

Dan let go of her hand. "Mmm, hence the Mrs Thatcher masks, go on," he said, coldly.

"Oh my God, I just got so immersed in it all. I was in way over my head, but Mark and Daddy would not let me out of my 'duty' as they called it."

"Ciara," Dan interjected. "Did you and Mark have anything to do with the Tower Hill bombing?"

Ciara put her head in her hands. "That we did. We didn't want to kill anyone though, just to cause disruption. Mark called the police station in Bishopsgate with a coded warning from a payphone in The Crispin when you were playing shoot pool.

"And to think it was *you* that nearly died. Neither Mark nor I have ever killed anyone, that I swear. We watched the melee from afar and mingled with the rest of the office when the evacuation started. We knew precisely the time the bomb would explode and neither of us had seen you come out. And we knew you were there because we'd seen you arrive in a taxi. I was terrified that you were going to die and got Mark to look for you. Thank God you survived."

"I've seen the guns in his desk, Ciara. They look like the same guns I found next to your bed last night. And I've seen those Thatcher masks in yours. Is there an attack planned for tonight? Why else would Mark have his dinner jacket clobber in his drawer?"

This time he was gripping her arms firmly. She took her time to respond. Her eyes glistened.

"I-I couldn't go through-through with it," she stammered. "It was going to be worse than before – so much worse. There were going to be casualties."

"Is everything alright in here?" said the Ward Sister in a curious tone. Dan got to his feet and put his hand gently on the nurse's shoulder as he led her outside the room.

"You'd better call the Police, Sister," he told her in a low tone. "There's going to be an IRA attack in London tonight, and our patient in there knows plenty about what's being planned."

The Sister went white and scuttled off to find a telephone. Dan returned to Ciara's room and shut the door behind him.

"Ok, so it's due to go ahead," he confirmed. "And it's looking very grave. But that still doesn't explain why you tried killing yourself. And what are you saying? I'm assuming that you're intending there to be mass casualties?"

"Dan, I know I've done some terrible things, but I couldn't be involved in this. I couldn't bring myself to be any part in hurting you. You'll not be wanting me now of course, but the truth is I love you. I've loved you since I thought we might have lost you in the Tower Bridge attack.

"Last night, directly before I took the pills, I called the police. I don't have the coded password that we use, and besides, there won't be one used tonight anyway. Mark and Daddy have a table for six of them – they think I'm coming with you. Mark briefed me this morning when he gave me my revolvers. They want me to be armed but not to take part in the attack myself. I'm just supposed to be telling them if I see anyone looking at them suspiciously.

"All six of them will be armed and will start shooting randomly at some point in the evening. They want me to leave just before the attack and drive a white van, which Mark has left outside my flat, to pick them up afterwards. I've told all this the police, but they don't know if I'm a crank or not. They probably won't believe me anyway. If they do prevent it somehow or even cancel the event altogether, the cell will eventually find out who exposed the plot, and my life won't be worth living anyway."

She was interrupted by two uniformed police officers and a WPC entering the room.

"We'd like you to wait outside please Sir," one of them said to Dan. "Our Inspector, DCI Logan, wishes to ask you some questions."

An armed constable stood by the door of the room, and an older man in a raincoat greeted Dan.

"DCI Derek Logan, Flying Squad" he introduced himself, shaking Dan's hand. "I think we'd better have a little chat."

The DCI and Dan took the lift down to the hospital exit. Logan offered Dan a cigarette, which he gratefully accepted. The DCI told Dan that his office had received a call from a woman the previous night but had decided it was probably a hoax as the caller was both drunk and had no coded password. Despite this, they had informed the general manager of the Grosvenor House Hotel of the call and suggested they upped security for the dinner, just in case. Two plain clothed policemen had been ordered to remain discreetly near the entrance of the hotel. The call from the hospital, however, had put them on red alert.

The DCI asked Dan to remain in the foyer of the hospital and wait for him to interview Miss Ciara Rogers. After that they were to pay a visit, not to the police station but to, as the DCI described it, "an office near Waterloo."

The "office in Waterloo" was actually an Italian café. Dan was surprised that at 11am the sign on the door said 'CLOSED'. There were three men inside, two seated drinking coffee and an elderly Italian man behind the counter.

The Italian man unlocked the door. "Eh Senor Logan, what do I get you an' yor fren'?" he greeted. "The others are 'ere."

"What do you fancy, sir?" the DCI asked Dan as he slipped the Italian man an envelope. Dan ordered a plain coffee. He noticed that the DCI hadn't paid for the coffees, nor the sandwich that Logan had ordered for himself. A police car with two constables within was parked directly outside the café.

This is an arrangement, thought Dan as Logan guided him to the table with the two other men.

"Mr Perry," said Logan. "These are gentlemen from MI5. I'm going to let them take over from here."

The MI5 officers spent nearly two hours grilling Dan. He explained everything from his relationships with Ciara and Mark, omitting only the insider dealing incident, to meeting Kelvin O'Brien in the pub at Cheltenham. He told them about the finding the masks in Ciara's drawer and the revolvers in Mark's. It seemed that they were already well aware of Kelvin's activities and had Mark on their radar but were less sure about Ciara.

Dan related everything that Ciara had told him from her hospital bed only hours earlier. He then went on to explain his relationship with the Archer brothers and how it had led to his invitation to the Grosvenor House Hotel that night.

Throughout the two hours they were in the café, one of the three men regularly went to a back room with their Motorola phones, the size of bricks. Dan vowed to get one for himself, if and when this nightmare ever came to an end.

"The dinner is going ahead," said the more senior of the MI5 officers.

Dan was incredulous. "How is the dinner going ahead when we know that there could be mass casualties tonight? I don't get it."

DCI Logan answered for the MI5 agents. "Let me explain. You don't have to be there, Danny boy, and it won't be any fun if you are, I can assure you, but you won't be in any danger. The SAS will be all over these murderous bastards, and they'll be nicked before you can say Jack Robinson.

"We wouldn't mind if you were there however. We know

Kelvin's appearance but aren't so sure of Mark's. You'll have a tiny microphone attached to your jacket, and anything you say will be picked up by all of the gentlemen of the SAS on surrounding tables. And guess what?" The DCI grinned. "I'll be your date tonight, not the lovely Miss Rogers."

Dan didn't need more convincing. He'd been this far; now it was time to see the end of this episode in his life. He agreed to meet Logan outside Sinclair Bank at 6pm, then caught a cab back to his home on Fulham Road. He picked up his dinner jacket, shirt, and bowtie whilst the cab waited at the curb, and returned to the city.

Logan was waiting for him as planned. He was driving a blue Ford Sierra and was immaculately dressed, hardly recognisable from his earlier attire of jeans and leather jacket.

A traffic warden approached the Ford Sierra and peered inside the car, indicating for Logan to wind down the window.

"You can't park here Sir, you're on a double yellow," the young man said.

Logan reached inside his jacket pocket and showed the warden his ID. "Police business, son," he dismissed. The traffic warden continued on his way and Dan, having spotted the car, climbed into the passenger seat.

"Grosvenor House Hotel, please, driver," Dan joked, making light of the situation that lay ahead.

"The Grosvenor House it is, sir," Logan smirked back.

Toxic Options

Chapter Fifteen

4pm, the same day

The white van arrived at the cheap hotel. Mark O'Brien parked directly outside on a yellow line. The men exited the van armed with their suitcases, each of them feeling the adrenalin gushing through them as the hour approached. Their trepidation. The imminent terror. Their responsibility for the forthcoming disaster. Revenge. All for the cause. Soldiers, not terrorists, as they knew the British newspapers would refer to them the following day.

"If you gentlemen would like to leave your luggage down here, I'll have your suitcases and bags taken to your rooms," said Eddie, the young manager of the insalubrious hotel in Earls Court, chosen two days earlier by Kelvin O'Brien.

Six new guests were now standing in reception and Eddie handed them three sets of keys. They'd booked three double rooms for one night in the name of Mr Regan.

"We'll not be needing yer to do that young man, thank you," said Kelvin O'Brien, nodding at the bags, before continuing, "Ok lads, let's get our gear to the rooms and reconvene in the dining room over there in thirty minutes."

He looked at Eddie and offered his hand to shake, which Eddie did. In the palm of O'Brien's hand was a £10 note, bribing Eddie to keep his mouth shut. "You won't mind us havin' a private meetin' in your dining room for a couple of hours or so, will you

[153]

son?"

"Pleased to help, Mr Regan," said Eddie, who was only too pleased to comply, especially as the room was unlikely to be needed by other guests until dinner. Tea was not on the agenda here, as most of the foreign tourists preferred to venture into central London for tea at one of the grand hotels. He'd cast his eye over this rather intimidating man and his colleagues, or 'business partners', as O'Brien had referred to them, and felt uncomfortable in their presence. There was something sinister about them, something he couldn't quite put his finger on. Still, it was business much needed by the hotel, and he was happy to take O'Brien's £10 considering he'd have let them have the room to themselves anyway.

The most senior of the men, Mr Regan, had reserved the rooms two nights earlier and said that he'd be paying himself in cash. Eddie wondered what sort of line they were in.

It was 4.30pm now, and the only guests currently in the hotel were the new intake of Irishmen, who'd commenced their meeting soon after taking their luggage upstairs to their rooms. All the others had ventured off sometime after breakfast.

Disturbing his thoughts, the phone rang. It was the local council asking if it would be ok to send a couple of firemen around to check for any fire hazards in the hotel. The councillor asked how many guests they had staying and how many of them were inside the hotel at that particular moment. Unusual for this time of day.

Eddie answered the questions and gave his permission, not

that he felt he had much choice in the matter, yet was surprised to welcome the firemen, in full uniform, only a few minutes after putting down the receiver.

The firemen asked him for the master key allowing them access to each room within the hotel. Eddie pondered the request uneasily. He didn't think that Mr Regan and his men would be entirely happy should they finish their business early and find someone checking their rooms. Maybe the other guests would care rather less?

Still, this was merely a safety issue, and safety was in all of the client's interests. Besides, he knew that Mr Regan's meeting was due to continue for at least another hour, and therefore none of them would be any the wiser.

Having checked the firemen's IDs, Eddie was asked by one of them to see the booking records. As the names were looked over, Eddie was asked, much to his surprise, if he could ascertain what dialect or nationality the guests were, particularly those that were currently in the dining room.

After Eddie had replied "Definitely Irish," the firemen asked that he leave them to their own devices.

Why did they need to see the booking records? he thought, but said nothing and complied with the request.

The firemen took half an hour to do their check and left, driving off in a red Voltzwagen Golf. Eddie thought no more of it. Routine checks by order of the council were part of regular hotel life, particularly in small hotels where hygiene and fire risks were likely to be more prevalent than at the bigger London hotels.

Half an hour earlier, Kelvin O'Brien had sat down at a table in the dining room surrounded by five members of the cell. Six Irishmen dressed in dinner jackets. Each had in front of them a photocopied floor plan of The Grosvenor House Hotel, showing both the large reception area and the Great Room itself, where they were due to convene that evening for the glittering racing dinner planned for that evening.

The floor plan had been constructed by Kelvin's son, Mark, who had checked in for an overnight stay at The Grosvenor House two weeks earlier. Mark had posed as a tourist and had not been interrupted when he had taken dozens of snaps of the 'architecture' from his polaroid camera.

These photographs were now being examined in great detail by the other five men in the room. They depicted the entrance from Park Lane, the lobby, the reception desk, the staircase, the lifts, and the bar. A Christmas function had been planned in The Great Room on the evening of Mark's impromptu visit and he'd eagerly taken the opportunity to photograph the table layout and various exits. He'd even ascertained which table they would be sitting at.

Kelvin O'Brien led the meeting. There were to be two plans. The first would involve them making the attack in the Great Room itself.

"Me daughter, Ciara, will be on table 23 with a guy from her work and our old friends the Archer brothers. After tonight, they'll wish they could have settled for a kicking and the hundred grand we relieved of them that night in Walthamstow a few years back.

"She will be armed but won't be involved in the attack. The other guests on table 23 will know that she works with Mark. If she spots anything untoward, any suspicious looks, anything, she'll come over to our table and tell Mark, who will be sitting next to me. In that event we may go earlier than planned.

"An award is due to be made at around 9pm to the leading trainer and jockey of the year. The lights will be dimmed before the presentation is made, at least that's what happened last year. That's when we start shooting. She'll make herself scarce before we open fire.

"We fire non-stop for ten seconds, killing at random, simultaneously making our way to the separate exits." He pointed to the floor plan, which detailed which of the exits each gunman would be leaving by.

"Plan B is the back up plan. We are unlikely to meet any trouble on our way to, or going into, the hotel. The security was shit last year. God knows, they still haven't learned from Brighton," said O'Brien, referring to the IRA attack on The Grand Hotel in Brighton at the Conservative Party conference three years earlier.

He continued, "The time that we could possibly encounter resistance is at the reception. If we're in the lobby, ok, which will be

[157]

full of guests, and anything goes wrong, then we open fire there and then on my command.

"We'd much prefer Plan A, as the guests will be sat down, away from us, and concentrating on the awards ceremony on the stage. However, in either case after the attack we'll make our way as quick as lightnin' to the van, which will be parked on Hill Street just up the road. Me daughter, Ciara, was fully briefed yesterday morning and will be driving, isn't that right Mark?"

Kevin O'Brien looked expectantly at his son, who nodded.

"Yes Daddy, I briefed her with all the instructions yesterday when I gave her her weapons, and she knows where I've hidden the keys to the van."

"You're a good lad Marky, that you are, son," replied his father before pointing out the location on a map and exactly where the white van would be parked. "From there we'll be driven to a different location; the other side of the park, where another vehicle will be awaiting us. Hopefully we can cause as much damage as possible in the hotel without capture.

"We do not under any circumstances return here. After this, you'll return to your rooms, arm yourselves, and leave the suitcases behind. We'll leave here at six o'clock and park the van on Hill Street. Fifteen minutes and we're on our way boys. Any questions?"

On the other side of London another meeting was in place.

Dan Perry was in a sweat, despite the cold December evening. He spoke to Logan. "Mark O'Brien was in the office earlier but unsurprisingly had left before I got there. Apparently he left shortly before twelve. One of my traders said he looked very distracted and didn't trade at all – spent all morning on the phone."

Dan turned to the Detective Inspector and confessed, "I'm shitting myself, Derek."

"You must stay calm, son," replied DCI Logan. "Since you went back to the office earlier, I've been working my arse off – we've had a stroke of luck too. Everything is under control. We're on table 23, they are on table 29. Each table for six surrounding table 29 will be exclusively filled by the highest trained soldiers in the land. The SAS, MI5, and my department are all over it.

"We even know where the cell is. And I mean now, right now. We had a tip off. A white van in Earls Court got given a parking ticket directly outside a hotel at around 4pm. Within half an hour, it's only come up on our system as the same vehicle used by the IRA on an armed robbery on a couple of bookies a few years back.

"MI5 were crawling all over the hotel within minutes. Posed as firemen doing a routine safety check. It was the first one they checked. We think the terror cell were there at the same time having a meeting. My lads picked up on it straight off. MI5 are following said white van as we speak."

At 7pm, Joss and Wayne Archer plus an assortment of their guests stood in the main bar located directly next door to the Great Room. Joss had had a few already, not just back in his Walthamstow local but a few of the 'free' glasses of Champagne being liberally offered in reception of the Grosvenor House Hotel by the waiters and waitresses.

"Fancy a lager, Sir Marcus?" he offered. Then, turning to Diana, Marcus's wife, "'Ere luv, martini and black?" He grinned as he handed over £20 to the barman. "Bottle of Magnum bubbly please, old mate."

Joss wasn't sure who looked more embarrassed, the Holdernesses' or the barman.

"Now come on Archer, you old bugger," boomed Captain Neville Taylor, jovially slapping Wayne across the back as he approached the throng. "We line your pockets all year and this is a chance to pay us a little back. It's not called Magnum, it's Moët, but we want a magnum of that!"

Diana shrieked with laughter. Joss reached for another £20 and handed it over the bar. "Fucking toffs, eh? It's free in reception." He winked at the barman with a broad grin. *A White Christmas* by Bing Crosbie hummed in the background.

The white van had parked in Hill Street. Mark was annoyed not to see Ciara there. She's said she'd be waiting for them. Still, she knew where he'd hidden the keys – on the top of the back left wheel, as they'd discussed yesterday.

No doubt she'd decided to go straight to the hotel with that tosser Dan and his party, he thought sourly. Still, he was sure she'd follow instructions and make her excuses to leave prematurely. He was slightly uneasy at how reticent she'd been about the attack, but she'd accepted the guns he brought to her and appeared to absorb all of his instructions.

Anyway, there was no point in waiting for her. She'd be there waiting for them when the deed had been done.

On Kelvin O'Brien's instructions, each of the terrorists carried their weapons in the inside pockets of their dinner jackets. Not that they had much choice, as none wore overcoats to protect themselves from the bite of the cold December chill. Coats were a liability – no point in risking themselves being spotted by one of those thenian British coat rack attendants at the hotel, a Mauser being noticed perchance as the attendant handed over a receipt. Coats would not be for collecting tonight.

Tonight was about execution and escape only. Triumph for the cause, and disaster for those that were the enemies of Ireland. Mark remembered Dan Perry talking of triumph and disaster at Cheltenham. How shallow was that? A poor little rich kid with a gambling problem. And shortly to be a poor, dead, little rich kid.

The Irishmen walked into the lobby of the Grosvenor House Hotel and swiftly split to different parts of the reception area. There must have well over 200 people in attendance.

The noise level was rising approaching 7.45pm. It was nearly time for dinner. Everyone was still in the reception area.

"Daddy, I'm gonna stick my face into the Great Room – back in a jiffy," said Mark, ignoring the waitress that tried offering him a glass of champagne.

He walked through the turning door that led into the Great Room. Empty. Silent in the huge room but noisy behind.

Mark surveyed the beautifully decorated tables with white tablecloths. The room was relatively dark too, the light mainly coming from candles within the holders adorning each table. The room shimmered and sparkled. This felt surreal. A spectacular Christmas event in a London hotel, soon to turn to horror. He looked for table 29. It appeared to be in the ideal spot to conduct the massacre.

Suddenly, he smelled behind him a strong smell of cigar smoke. He turned to find the trainer, Captain Neville Taylor, standing right behind him.

"Surveilling the scenery, old man?" asked the captain. "We've just been given the all-clear to go through. By the way, I don't suppose you have a light? This damn thing is cutting out." He gestured to the dying embers of his cigar.

Mark was thrown. He was in the middle of his reconnaissance mission pending an attack that would frame the headlines of the world's newspapers the following day, and here was this oaf, asking him for a light. He was flustered but knew he must stay as calm as possible.

"No problem, Captain Taylor. Nice winner you had last Saturday," said Mark whilst clumsily looking for his lighter. He quickly checked his trouser pockets, but to no avail. Just some cash and some cigarettes. He knew that he had the lighter on him somewhere. He'd had a fag on his walk from the van on Hill Street.

It was then that he made his mistake. He just needed to get this idiot off his back as quickly as possible. He opened the inside pocket of his dinner suit, and Captain Neville Taylor spotted it in a flash. He'd handled a Mauser many times in his army days.

"What the fuck are you doing with that?" he demanded, stiffening. He spotted the look of terror on Mark's face.

Mark reached for his revolver but was far too slow. Captain Taylor's instinct as a soldier had made him alert to danger. He lunged and gripped the other man's wrist before Mark's fingers even touched the weapon.

The two men grappled, and the elder man's grip loosened. Mark used his spare hand and successfully pulled out the Colt from his other jacket pocket.

"You fucking bastard! You die now, you fucking British army bastard," shouted Mark as he swung the other weapon to point towards the captain's head.

From nowhere, a man behind the two wrestling men smashed a candlestick holder into Mark O'Brien's head and the Colt revolver fell from the Irishman's hand. Mark let out a long groan and fell to the floor, now passed out.

The captain barked, "Get help, man, right now," to his saviour, who he still hadn't had a chance to see. He turned Mark

O'Brien's unconscious body over and sat on him.

Joss Archer replied, "You hoorays never say thank you."

A waitress had seen the scene in the Great Room unfold, and before Joss had had a chance to alert the other partygoers, she had run into the reception area in a panic. Other party guests began to notice the trouble, and the screaming began.

An Irish cry of "Now, lads!" was inaudible to all amongst the ensuing mayhem. No sooner had Kelvin O'Brien screamed the order than he had been instantly overpowered by two of the other guests, who had barely left his side since he entered the hotel. He never had a chance. The same fate had met the four remaining gunmen within a split second.

The screaming and shouting and panic raged on as terrified guests tried to flee the hotel by whatever means possible. Inside, six men lay alive yet overpowered, now unarmed and handcuffed, with the weapons of the SAS trained on each of them.

Dan had hardly had a chance to say a word to his 'date', DI Logan. He was too nervous to speak.

Logan had explained to him in the car from the city that the SAS soldiers were marking the terrorists every move and had done so ever since the cell had stepped out of the hotel in Earls Court. The white van, linked by the Met's security systems to the provisional IRA, had been followed all the way to Hill Street and the cell followed to the entrance of the Grosvenor House Hotel. Logan had spent most of the journey from the city to Park Lane on his walkie talkie.

"I think it's time for you to go home now, son," Logan said to Dan. "Now that the military have done the dirty work, and pretty efficiently they did it too, I think you'll agree, it's time for my lads to take over. I'll be in touch shortly.

"Now, I'd go and have a stiff drink if I were you. Thanks for your help, Danny boy. You helped prevent a catastrophe, and we now have six IRA Commandos in our keep, shortly to be under lock and key. We'll get a load of intelligence from these bastards; you mark my words."

Dan didn't doubt it.

A voice rattled over Logan's walkie talkie and the policeman's hand went out to Dan. Dan knew it was time for him to go. He shook Logan's hand and left the hotel, walking the mile and half back to his Fulham Road flat.

Toxic Options

About the Author

The author was born in London and worked as a city trader and broker between 1981-2004. He subsequently ran a recruitment company for 10 years and is a qualified freelance journalist.

He married Michelle in 1999.

They live in Fulham, London, with their cat, Izzy.

Printed in Great Britain
by Amazon